D1322411

ACROSS THE DIVIDE

Praise for *Across The Divide*:

'A compelling historical novel set against the backdrop of the
Dublin Lockout of 1913 ... The author breathes life into characters
who in lesser hands could become stereotypes.
A skilful, satisfying read.'
Inis Magazine

'Will have young readers eagerly turning the pages to see what
happens next. Highly recommended.' *Bookfest*

'An intelligent look at a particularly turbulent piece of Irish history
from a young person's viewpoint.' *Books Ireland*

'The atmosphere of a troubled Dublin city awash with tension and
poverty is excellently captured.' *Irish Examiner*

Brian Gallagher is a full-time writer whose plays and short stories have been produced in Ireland, Britain and Canada. He has written extensively for radio and television and for many years was one of the script-writers on RTÉ's *Fair City*.

He followed the success of *Across The Divide* with another historical novel for young readers, *Taking Sides*, where the friendship between Annie Reilly and Peter Scanlon is severely tested when Peter becomes involved in rebel activities as the country is heading into Civil War.

Brian has collaborated with composer Shaun Purcell on the musical, *Larkin*, for which he wrote the book and lyrics, and on *Winds of Change* for RTÉ's Lyric FM. He lives with his family in Dublin.

ACROSS
THE
DIVIDE

BRIAN GALLAGHER

THE O'BRIEN PRESS
DUBLIN

First published 2010 by The O'Brien Press Ltd,
12 Terenure Road East, Rathgar, Dublin 6, Ireland.
Tel: +353 1 4923333; Fax: +353 1 4922777
E-mail: books@obrien.ie; Website: www.obrien.ie
Reprinted 2011, 2012.

ISBN:978-1-84717-172-6

British Library Cataloguing-in-Publication Data
A catalogue record for this title is available from the British Library

3 4 5 6
12 13 14 15

Editing, typesetting, layout and design: The O'Brien Press Ltd
Cover images courtesy of iStockphoto
Printed and bound by CPI Group (UK) Ltd, Croydon, CR0 4YY
The paper used in this book is produced using pulp from managed forests

The O'Brien Press receives assistance from

DEDICATION:

To Pat and Mary.
Thanks for all the friendship and support.

ACKNOWLEDGEMENTS:

My sincere thanks go to Michael O'Brien for his initial sugges-
tion that I write a children's historical novel, and to my editor,
Mary Webb, for her many insightful contributions.

I'm greatly indebted to Annie-Rose O'Mahony and Sean
Pardy, two well-read young people who generously took the
time to read the first draft and share their observations with me.

My thanks also go to Dave 'Doc' O'Connor and Pauline Pardy
for their assistance, and to Hugh Mc Cusker for his eagle-eyed
proof-reading.

And finally, but most significantly of all, my deepest thanks go
to my family, Miriam, Orla and Peter, for all the ways in which
they support me.

Brian Gallagher.

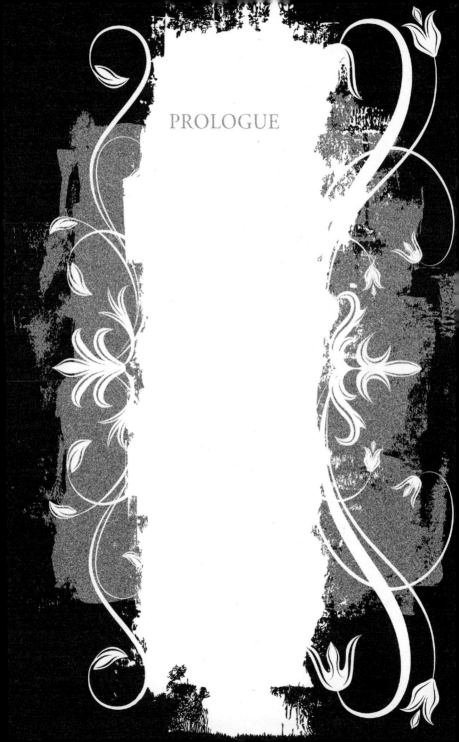

PROLOGUE

31 AUGUST 1913
SACKVILLE STREET, DUBLIN.

Liam knew that he shouldn't be here. It was no place for a ten-year-old boy; any adult would tell you that. But he hadn't asked an adult. He had just sneaked into town without anyone knowing. Because really, he *had* to be here. Today's meeting in the city's main street was too exciting to miss, and he looked forward to telling his friend Nora all about his adventures later on.

Last night Liam had heard his mother saying that the police had banned Jim Larkin, the leader of the city's striking workers, from addressing the people of Dublin. But Larkin had insisted that he would appear in Sackville Street at half past one today, police or no police. Liam had no idea how Larkin was going to do it, and neither, it seemed, had anybody else, but the street was thronged with people eager to see what would happen.

Even though he was fairly tall for a ten-year-old, Liam found it hard to see across Sackville Street as he stood at the base of Nelson's Pillar, the high column topped by a statue of Lord Nelson that Ma said was the exact centre of Dublin. The thought of his mother made him feel guilty. She'd be worried if she knew that he was here alone and surrounded by grown-ups. And there *was* a funny mood in the crowd, a slightly frightening sense that something, *anything* could suddenly happen. But things that were frightening were sometimes exciting too, and Liam told himself that what his mother didn't know needn't worry her, and that if his hero, Mr Larkin, wasn't afraid, then he wouldn't be either.

There were hundreds of policemen on duty, and as Liam moved down the street towards the General Post Office he noticed how angry some of them seemed, fingering their batons and looking suspiciously at the people who spilled off the footpaths and onto the street.

The crowd itself was an odd mixture, with Larkin's supporters, mostly working men in their caps and Sunday-best jackets, mingling with well-dressed people coming from Mass in the nearby pro-Cathedral. Liam checked the time on the big clock mounted on the wall above a nearby shop. It was twenty-nine minutes past one. Only one minute to go, and still no sign of Jim Larkin. It would be really disappointing if he didn't show up, yet with policemen stationed at every corner it was hard to see how the leader of the striking workers could keep his promise. But he *always* kept his promises, Liam's father had said last night, you could count on it.

Thinking of his father, Liam glanced around nervously. As a loyal supporter of Larkin, Da was bound to be somewhere in the crowd. And Liam would be in serious trouble with him if he was spotted here. He would have loved to come into town today with him, but there was no question of his father bringing his son to a meeting banned by the police.

'Make way there, make way,' cried a big police sergeant, and Liam was jostled forward as a line of officers pushed the crowd back to allow a carriage to draw up outside the Imperial Hotel, directly across the road from the General Post Office.

Through a gap in the crowd Liam watched as a bearded, elderly man and an expensively dressed woman emerged from the carriage and made for the hotel entrance. Liam felt a surge of annoyance. Why should everyone else be pushed out of the way just because somebody rich wanted to enter the hotel? It wasn't that he had anything against the lady or the man – whom he now saw was stooped and slow-moving – but why did the police have to be so rough with everyone else? Da said that the police were completely on the side of the employers. So pushing the ordinary people back was a way of showing them who was boss.

Liam felt a tap on his shoulder.

'You shouldn't be here, sonny,' said a voice in a strong country accent.

Liam looked up to see a tall policeman looking down at him.

'Be on off home with you now,' said the man gruffly.

Part of Liam wanted to say 'Dublin *is* my home,' but it wouldn't be a good idea to give cheek to a policeman. He hesitated, reluctant to argue back, but not wanting to give in at once.

'Well, what are you waiting for?'

'Jim Larkin,' answered Liam, the smart answer slipping out before he could stop himself.

The policeman's face darkened. 'Don't give me lip, you little pup!' The man took a step nearer, and Liam drew back.

There was a sudden roar from the crowd.

'Larkin! It's Larkin!'

They began cheering wildly and pointing to a balcony on the first floor of the Imperial Hotel. To Liam's relief, the policeman turned away and began pushing his way towards the hotel.

Liam stood on tiptoe to see the figure on the balcony. It couldn't be! But it was: the elderly gentleman who had walked so shakily from the carriage was now standing erect and proud. It was Jim Larkin!

'Workers of Dublin, I said I'd be here, and here I am!'

The crowd went mad, and Liam found himself cheering loudly along with the people around him.

There was a sudden surge as police converged on the hotel, and Liam knew it wouldn't be long before Larkin was arrested. Sure enough, before Larkin could say much more he was pulled back off the balcony. But the briefness of the appearance didn't matter to Liam or to the people in the street. Their hero had outfoxed his enemies once again and coolly kept his promise to appear, right under their noses.

Liam ran forward, wanting to see Larkin in the flesh as he was led away. The people behind him surged forward too, but were stopped by the police, who had formed a cordon around the hotel. Standing as close to the line of policemen as he dared, his heart pounding, Liam saw a flurry of activity at the door of the Imperial. Then an officer in command of a group of uniformed policemen bundled Larkin out the door and towards a carriage.

Before Liam knew what he was doing, he called out, 'Well done, Mr Larkin!'

The tall union leader, still wearing the false beard that had been part of his disguise, turned his head towards the voice. Locking eyes briefly with Liam, he winked, and then was thrust into the carriage.

Winked at by Jim Larkin! Liam could hardly believe it. Wouldn't that be something to tell Da, if he dared!

As the carriage pulled away, scuffling broke out on the roadway near the hotel entrance. There was a cry of 'Baton charge!' and within seconds there was chaos. The policemen who had earlier been fingering their batons now suddenly wielded them savagely. People screamed in pain, and men fell to the ground, blood streaming from their heads and faces. Liam felt his stomach tighten in fear and he tried to run in the opposite direction, but was forced back by the crowd behind him who were being batoned by police officers advancing from the direction of Nelson's Pillar.

Turning on his heel, Liam ran as best he could down the middle of the road, dodging the bodies of those who had already fallen. He couldn't believe that the police were attacking everyone in sight. But something had been unleashed today, and nobody was safe, not even a boy like himself.

As if to prove it, a nearby policeman, having just felled a middle-aged man with a sickening blow from his baton, swung around and flailed at Liam. Dodging from an attack that might have split his head, Liam still caught part of the blow on his shoulder, and he cried out in pain.

Before the man could swing again, Liam ducked in panic under his outstretched arm and ran on down the street. Soon he was near the turn for Sackville Place, where he attended choir practice with Nora two nights a week. There was a laneway that ran off Sackville Place and parallel to Marlborough Street; if he could just make it to there, maybe he could escape from the horror of the riot.

He ran to the corner of Sackville Place and turned into it, then stopped dead. Mounted policemen were advancing towards him, reaching down from their saddles and felling anyone within range of their batons.

Liam turned and fled, the cries of those being pursued by the horsemen ringing in his ears. Sackville Street was now like a battlefield, but Liam didn't hesitate and ran diagonally across the broad thoroughfare, heading for Prince's Street and the alley at its far end that would take him to Middle Abbey Street and safety.

Lots of other people were running in the same direction, and he couldn't see clearly what lay ahead. Suddenly the crowd halted in disarray. Liam heard the order 'Reserves advance!', and the people in front of him milled about, trying to reverse direction as the reserve body of police officers was unleashed.

Really frightened now, Liam hesitated, not knowing what to do. People all around him began to be hit, trapped as they were in front and rear. Liam crouched and raised his arms to try to protect his head. A heavy hand spun him around, then a baton crashed into his temple. For a split second he saw a blinding light, then he fell to the ground and everything faded to darkness.

PART ONE

SEEDS OF TROUBLE

Chapter 1

MARCH 1913

FR MATHEW HALL, DUBLIN.

Nora felt a surge of panic. She searched through the sheet music in her leather satchel but couldn't find the page she wanted. *It must be here somewhere,* she told herself, *it just has to be!* She went through the music again, sheet by sheet, hoping to find the page she needed, perhaps stuck to another page. But there was no mistake – it was missing.

Nora felt a sinking sensation. This should have been a special day. She was dressed in her new green velvet dress, and her mother had bought matching ribbons for her hair, but now things had gone badly wrong. Desperately wanting to keep the feeling of panic at bay, Nora closed her eyes and breathed deeply, doing the relaxation exercise her singing teacher had taught her.

Normally Nora loved the atmosphere backstage at a *feis*, waiting in the wings with the other competitors. She liked the special dusty smell that you only got in theatres, and she enjoyed the excitement of competing, and the fun you could have with the other contestants. Today everyone in the under-twelve age group had to sing Gounod's '*Ave Maria*', and Nora had been happy with her performance. She was hoping to score well with her selected piece, Gilbert and Sullivan's 'Take a Pair of Sparkling Eye*s*'. But without the sheet music for the pianist who accompanied each performer, what was she going to do?

And what would her mother say? Although Nora had been singing at *feiseanna* since she was six, it was only recently that she had convinced her mother that at ten years of age she was old enough to look after her own music.

Even as she took slow deep breaths, Nora's mind was racing. Maybe she could sing another song? A different song wouldn't be as well rehearsed as 'Take a Pair of Sparkling Eye*s*', and would lessen her chances of winning, especially today when she was competing against Kathleen Brogan, who performed in all the *feiseanna*, and who won lots of prizes. Still, singing a different piece would be better than going out to the auditorium and confessing her mistake to her mother. Except that if she sang something else she would be questioned, wouldn't she? *After so much practice, Nora, why did you change songs?*

She could claim that she had switched songs because one of the other contestants had already sung 'Take a Pair of

Sparkling Eyes'. He was a boy of about her own age and he had performed it very well.

A sudden thought struck her. Nora opened her eyes and searched among the waiting competitors for the boy who had sung her song. He must be new to the circuit; she had never seen him at any other *feiseanna*. There he was! He looked relaxed as he sat on a chair, reading a comic book and pushing back a strand of wavy brown hair that had fallen down onto his forehead. His hob-nailed boots were old, but well polished.

Could she do it? Could she ask a boy she had never met to lend her the music? The more she hesitated, the more unreasonable it seemed. After all, they *were* competing against each other. Could she really ask for his help – in her efforts to beat him? No, that wouldn't be fair. She would be in trouble now with her mother, with her singing teacher, with everyone! She had practised really hard for today, but it was all going wrong. Nora felt tears starting to well up in her eyes, though she tried to keep them at bay.

Just then the boy looked up from his comic and glanced towards her. He gave her a half-smile, his blue eyes friendly.

Nora immediately turned away. She rose quickly and made her way to a far corner of the theatre's wings, hoping that the boy hadn't noticed that she was upset. Taking out her handkerchief, she dabbed her eyes dry. There was no use feeling sorry for herself; she would just have to tell her mother the truth.

'It's only a song,' a voice said.

Nora turned to discover that the wavy-haired boy had followed her.

'I beg your pardon?'

'No good being upset. Just go on and do your best.'

So he *had* seen the tears forming in her eyes. And he thought she was upset at having to perform again.

'It's … it's not that,' she said.

'What is it then?'

Nora wasn't used to strangers being so blunt, yet she found herself answering openly.

'I forgot my music. Mummy will be really upset.'

'No music? Holy God!'

Nora was taken aback. She didn't know many boys, but those she had met didn't speak like this.

'Have you music for any other piece?' the boy asked.

'Yes, but I've practised "Take a Pair of Sparkling Eyes". So my mother will ask questions if I sing something else.'

'That's your piece? "Take a Pair of Sparkling Eyes"?'

'Yes.'

This was her opportunity. He was kind, he was friendly, there was a good chance he might help her. She looked at him, searching for the right words. But then she faltered, unable to find the nerve to ask.

'Sure, you're all right then,' the boy said. 'You can use mine.'

'I … I can't just take yours,' Nora said, feeling that polite-
ness demanded this.

'Fair enough. I'll sell it to you. Say, a tanner?'

Nora was a little bit shocked. Sixpence was a lot – more
than her entire weekly pocket money. On the other hand, the
sheet music would be a lifesaver.

'I don't have sixpence with me,' she explained, 'but–'

The boy burst out laughing. 'Will you get out of it! I'm only
messing.' He reached inside the cover of the comic book and
removed the music. 'Here, take it.'

'Even though we're rivals?'

'I want to win 'cause I'm the best, not 'cause you forgot
your music!'

The boy was grinning, and Nora found herself smiling
back. It was as though a weight had lifted from her, and she
felt a stab of affection for this slightly cocky, slightly rough,
but clearly generous boy.

'Thank you so much,' she said, taking the music.

'You're grand.'

'I … I don't even know your name.'

'Liam. Liam O'Meara.'

'Hello, Liam.' Nora held out her hand. 'I'm Nora Reynolds.'

'Well hello, Nora Reynolds,' he answered with a grin, then
he held out his hand, and Nora happily shook it.

＊　＊　＊

'Ladies and Gentlemen, it is my pleasant duty to announce the results of the Under-Twelve singing competition.'

Nora felt her pulses starting to race as the Master of Ceremonies spoke from the stage. Her mother reached out and squeezed Nora's hand encouragingly as they sat together in the auditorium. The standard had been high, but Nora felt that she had done well with 'Take a Pair of Sparkling Eyes'.

After the performance she had returned the sheet music to her new friend, Liam, and they had chatted easily together backstage until all the contestants were finished. She was surprised when Liam told her that he had come here on his own, his home in Phibsboro being only a short distance from the Fr Mathew Hall. Nora had never travelled to a *feis* on her own and was a bit envious of the amount of freedom that Liam seemed to enjoy. On the other hand, it meant that none of his family was here to support him. She found herself really curious about his world, which she suspected was very different to her own.

She could see him now, sitting on the end seat of a nearby row, and she gave him a quick wave. He smiled and gave a thumbs-up sign, then they both looked up to the stage as the MC unfolded the sheet of paper with the winners' names.

'In second place, the winner of the silver medal is Miss Kathleen Brogan.'

There was applause in which Nora and her mother joined politely. Nora was unsure whether to be pleased or not. No one really liked Kathleen Brogan, and it would have been nice to see her out of the medals for once. Still, she hadn't won the gold, so Nora still had a chance of beating her. She waited anxiously as Kathleen, all simpering smiles, mounted the stage and collected her medal. The MC consulted his list again. Nora could see Liam straining forward in his seat, and she hoped that the prize would go to him if she didn't win.

'In first place, the winner of the gold medal is …' The man paused dramatically, and Nora felt irritated by his self-satisfied smile as he made the contestants sweat it out. Eventually he looked out into the auditorium and called out the winner's name … 'Master Eamon Fitzgerald!'

Nora's heart sank. A thin boy with dark, curly hair approached the stage to claim his prize. He had sung well, and the judges must have felt that over the two pieces his was the highest standard. She was disappointed, but at least she had avoided getting into trouble, she would probably get a good written commendation from the judges, and she had made a new friend in Liam.

She looked over at him now, and he made a face at her as if to say, 'Oh well'.

She shrugged and smiled ruefully at him, then turned back as her mother spoke.

'That's disappointing, Nora.'

'Yes.'

'I thought you had a good chance of winning the gold.' Her mother made an effort to be cheerful. 'Well … maybe next time, dear.'

Nora gave her arm an affectionate squeeze. Despite being very strict about some things, her mother never scolded her after a competition or pointed out her faults, like she had heard some mothers doing.

Out of the corner of her eye, Nora saw Liam rising from his seat. He made his way in her direction and smiled as he reached her.

'I'll see you, Nora. I'm just going to get my letter from the judges and head off.'

'Right.' Nora felt torn. She had gotten to like him in the brief time that they had known each other, and she really ought to introduce him to her mother. But another part of her wanted him to go away as quickly as possible, in case he let slip about the sheet music.

Liam looked expectantly at her mother, and Nora knew that she had no choice.

'Mummy, I'd like you to meet Liam.'

Her mother held out her hand. 'How do you do, Liam?' she said as they shook hands.

'I'm grand. And yourself?'

Nora could see that her mother was slightly taken aback by Liam's response.

'I'm very well, thank you.'

'That's the best day you'll ever see.' Liam grinned. 'That's what my granny always says.'

'Indeed.'

'Anyway, I better run. See you at the next *feis*, Nora.'

'Yes, see you, Liam.'

He nodded to her mother. 'Nice meeting you.'

'You too.'

Nora was relieved that Liam had given nothing away, and she smiled as he gave her a conspiratorial wink before moving off.

'How did you come to meet this boy?' her mother asked.

'We, eh … we got chatting backstage,' Nora answered, wanting to avoid telling an outright lie.

'I don't wish to be harsh, dear, but he's not really our kind of person.' Her mother was speaking in the quiet but firm tone that she used when she felt strongly about something.

'I dare say he's a pleasant, friendly sort of boy. But it's better to choose friends from one's own background. Better all round, from his point of view as well as yours.'

Nora felt like asking how it could be better for Liam, or for her for that matter, if they weren't friends the next time they met at a *feis*, but she didn't argue. Her mother could be snobbish – much more so than Daddy – when speaking about poorer people. And she supposed that her family *was* reasonably wealthy. But why hold that against Liam?

Nora remembered how shocked she had been when her father had allowed her to come with him once on a visit to his company's wine vaults in Sheriff Street, in the city centre. She had seen filthy, barefoot children playing in the gutters, children who looked sick and hungry. Compared to them, Liam clearly came from a family that wasn't doing too badly.

Liam had saved her from big trouble, he had been good fun to talk to, and she was really glad she had met him. She would have to keep it a secret from her mother, but they *were* going to meet again, and when that happened they *would* still be friends.

Chapter 2

Liam was biding his time. If you wanted to get his da's approval for something, it was important to catch him in the right mood. Liam sat in a corner of the front room, pretending to read a library book, while his parents occupied the two slightly battered armchairs on either side of the fire.

Liam waited until his four sisters had gone to the kitchen, where nine-year-old Eileen – who was almost as good a cook as their mother – was helping the other girls to make apple tarts. His mother was sewing a dress for Peg, his little sister, while Da spoke excitedly about the latest conflict between Larkin's union and the employers.

By this stage Liam knew the arguments by heart: how Dublin had worse slums than Calcutta, how labourers desperate for work slaved for up to seventeen hours a day, how the dreaded disease of tuberculosis, or 'the consumption' as his granny called it, was fifty percent worse in Ireland than in England or Scotland because so many workers lived in filthy, crowded tenements.

He glanced over at his father and felt a sudden stab of pride at having a parent who was always willing to fight for the underdog.

'Jim Larkin is right, Kitty,' said his da. 'We've got to get off our knees. The bosses will walk on us till we do.'

'I know,' said his wife. 'But it's one thing to strike against your own boss. Joining other workers to go on strike against their employers, though …'

'It makes them take us seriously.'

'Maybe. But it's also made them band together against the workers. I hope the union hasn't bitten off more than it can chew.'

'Jim Larkin will see us right, never you fear.'

His father said it with conviction, and Ma seemed to accept the assurance, and returned her attention to her sewing. Then Da reached into his pocket and took out his pipe, and Liam felt the time had come to ask his question. He hesitated, anxious to get the tone just right. If he asked too casually his father might dismiss him. But if he made it sound like he was asking for something really big, his da might look at it seriously – and find a reason to say no.

Only one way to find out, Liam thought, as he put down his library book.

'Da?'

'Yes, son?'

'When I was at the *feis* I met a man called Brother Raymond.'

'Did you? And who's Brother Raymond when he's at home?'

'Billy,' said his wife chidingly, looking up from her sewing.

Ma was always very respectful of anything to do with religion. Da was a Catholic too, but he wasn't pious, and he disliked the kind of blatantly holy people he called 'craw-thumpers'.

'He's a Capuchin friar who's starting a new choir,' explained Liam. 'He heard me singing and asked if I'd like to join.'

'Did he now?' said Da, pressing the tobacco into the pipe with his thumb before looking enquiringly at Liam. 'And what did you say?'

'That I'd ask my parents.'

'Maybe *Brother Raymond* should have been the one to ask us.'

'Don't be like that, Billy,' said his wife. 'Picking Liam is a big compliment.'

'And what about you, Liam? Do you want to join?'

Liam nodded. 'It sounds good. He said he wants to make it into one of the best choirs in Dublin.'

His father seemed to consider this as he continued lighting his pipe, but Liam sensed that he wasn't quite convinced, and so he tried to sell the idea a bit more.

'A boy I met at the *feis* is in a choir in Rathmines. They sing at weddings and funerals; you can make a few bob from it.'

His father smiled as he drew on his pipe, and Liam felt his hopes rising.

'You're a right little moneybags, aren't you?'

Liam wasn't sure that this was a good response. 'I just thought I could bring in something for the family,' he said.

'Right.'

'So, can I go, Da?'

Liam waited anxiously as his father puffed vigorously to get the pipe going. Finally he lowered the pipe and looked at Liam.

'All right then. On one condition.'

'What?'

'They sing free of charge at my funeral.'

'Billy!' said Ma, but she was laughing even as she scolded him.

Liam laughed too. 'Thanks, Da,' he said, 'that's a deal!'

Usually, Nora loved Sundays with her family, especially lunchtime when they would all sit down together at the dining room table, with linen napkins, shining glasses and the best damask tablecloth. Cook made an extra effort for Sunday lunch: Beef Wellington, or poached salmon, roast stuffed chicken with delicious gravy – and always roast potatoes. Golden brown and crisp on the outside, but soft and floury in the middle, they were Nora's favourite food in the world.

Hazy April sunshine streamed in through the tall French windows as she sat between her two brothers, David and Peter, and finished her last roast potato. Despite the good food and the happy family atmosphere, Nora's mind was slightly clouded by outside events. She looked across the table at her father, hoping that he could put her mind at ease.

'Daddy, can I ask you something?'

'Of course, dear.'

'Why were the suffragettes put in jail?' Nora had heard about a group of women in London who called themselves suffragettes and who were demanding rights for women.

'They broke the law, Nora,' answered her father.

'How?'

'By agitating and protesting.'

Nora looked at him, not understanding what was actually wrong with that.

Her father must have realised that he hadn't explained enough, for now he put down his knife and fork and spoke patiently.

'You know that every few years the people elect a government?'

'Yes.'

'Well, the suffragettes are saying that every woman in the country should have a vote. Demanding it, in fact.'

'But, Daddy ... what's wrong with women voting?'

'Don't be stupid!' said her brother.

'Manners, David,' corrected their mother.

The best way to annoy her eight-year-old brother was to ignore him completely, and so Nora looked instead at her father, who smiled indulgently.

'That's not how things are done, Nora,' he said.

'Why not?'

'It's not a lady's place to get involved in such things,' said her mother.

'Miss Dillon says a girl should be free to pursue any goal,' answered Nora, quoting her teacher, whom all of the girls in school admired.

'Miss Dillon should have a care,' her mother said warningly. 'She's not employed to undermine the social order.'

Now Nora was sorry she had said anything. The last thing she wanted was to get her favourite teacher into trouble.

'These are not things for you to worry about, dear,' said her father soothingly. 'Time enough for all that when you're older. All right?'

'All right.'

But now Nora did have something to worry about. Suppose her mother wrote a letter of complaint about Miss Dillon? The nuns who ran Nora's convent school held all the power. If they weren't happy with a teacher they could dismiss her. And then there were the suffragettes. Easy enough for Daddy to say not to worry. *He* had a vote. Nora was determined that one day she too would vote, it was only fair. But the idea of being locked up in prison like the suffragettes was really frightening.

'Lemon meringue pie for dessert, Nora,' said her father with a smile.

She realised that he was trying to distract her, but she also knew that he meant it as a kindness.

'Great,' she answered, trying for a smile in return. But though she loved lemon meringue, she just made a show of pushing it around her plate when it came. Somehow she had lost her appetite.

Chapter 3

Liam set off excitedly for the first meeting of the choir. His family lived on a road of terraced cottages near where the Royal Canal branch line ended at Broadstone railway station, and he had allowed himself enough time to walk the short distance into the city centre. He made his way across Mountjoy Street, happily skipping from point to point over the cobblestones to keep his boots free of horse dung.

He skirted St Mary's Protestant Church, known locally as the Black Church. It was said that if you ran around the church three times at midnight you would meet the devil. Liam wasn't sure if he believed that – though he had no intention of ever testing it – but even on a bright spring evening like this he didn't linger at the Black Church.

He carried on towards Dorset Street, then stopped to watch as two tall police officers manhandled a prisoner out through the doorway of a foul-smelling nearby tenement. Their captive was a shabbily dressed man who was pasty-faced and gaunt-looking, but who still carried himself with an air of defiance.

A striker, Liam thought. He knew from listening to his father that the police were tracking down strikers to where they lived. And some of the constables weren't slow about handing out a beating. At least this man hadn't been beaten and still had his pride, Liam thought with relief, as he watched the prisoner being taken in the direction of Phibsboro police station.

Liam continued on towards town, going past the Rotunda Maternity Hospital where he and his four sisters had been born. He turned into the top of Sackville Street and walked down towards Nelson's Pillar, his mind on what lay ahead. He was flattered that Brother Raymond had picked him for this new choir. At the same time he was a little nervous. Who knew what it would be like practising with Brother Raymond? The Brother had seemed friendly and outgoing the day they had met at the *feis*. But maybe that was to get people to join. Maybe when you were a member he would be really strict, and quick to anger.

Caught up in his thoughts, Liam turned into Sackville Place, followed the house numbers, and suddenly found himself outside the building where the rehearsal was to be held. He hesitated a moment, then he readied himself, reached out and knocked firmly on the door.

❋ ❋ ❋

Nora's spirits lifted when she saw Liam entering the

rehearsal room. There were lots of young people here that Nora had never seen before, but several of the other contestants from last month's *feis* in the Fr Mathew Hall were also present, and she had hoped that Liam would be among those chosen for the new choir.

She wasn't quite sure why she was so pleased to see him. Part of it was how kind he had been over the sheet music, and he had been good fun. But there was also the fact that her mother had warned her off him, unfairly, Nora felt, and that gave being friends a certain thrill.

In fact, things generally were looking up. Her earlier fears that her mother might report Miss Dillon appeared to be unfounded. At home Mummy had said nothing more on the matter, and Miss Dillon continued to behave in the confident and inspiring way that the girls in school found so exciting.

And then there was tonight's breakthrough, when Nora had persuaded her parents to let her travel alone into town. She had pointed out that she was ten, she was responsible, she made her own way to school every day. It was a simple matter of going around the corner, catching a tram into town, attending the rehearsal and then getting another tram home. And, Eureka, her parents had actually accepted her arguments!

Nora had felt very grown up paying her own tram fare, and she had relished the sense of freedom as she travelled into the city centre on the upstairs section of the tram. Now she looked across the room and caught Liam's eye, and he smiled and approached her.

'Nora, how are you doin'?'

'Hello, Liam.'

'Got your sheet music tonight?' he asked with a grin.

'Sheet music?' Nora felt a tiny stab of anxiety. 'Were we supposed to bring some?'

'Relax, I'm only messing.' He looked around. 'I see a few faces from the Fr Mathew.'

'Yes,' answered Nora, 'Brother Raymond must have been picking and choosing.'

'No sign of your woman, Kathleen what's-her-face?'

Nora laughed, never having heard this expression before. 'Kathleen Brogan?'

'Yeah, Little Miss Perfect. I'm surprised she wasn't picked.'

'I'd say she was,' Nora said.

'And what, she's too full of herself to join?'

Nora knew that it wasn't very polite to talk about people this way, but she couldn't help but enjoy Liam's lack of regard for Kathleen Brogan, who *was* a bit stuck-up.

'Probably. She's already in a couple of choirs, she doesn't need this.'

'And what about you?' asked Liam.

'I'm in the school choir. But that's sort of like school, so I thought this might be more fun.'

'Let's hope so.'

'Are you in any other choir?'

He shook his head. 'No. Sure it's only in the last year that I've started singing much.'

'Really?'

'Yeah. How long are you doing it?'

'I've been having lessons since I was around six.'

'My da couldn't afford lessons,' said Liam without any hint of discomfort. 'There's a new teacher in my school, though, and he said I've a good voice. He's been teaching me a bit – it was through him I entered the *feis*.'

'I'm glad. Well, as long as you never beat me to a prize!'

'Only a matter of time,' answered Liam with a grin.

'You think so?'

'Of course. Meantime though, we might have a bit of fun together in this choir. What do you think?'

'I'd like that,' said Nora, feeling as though they had made a pact.

'Of course,' Liam added, 'that's always providing your man Brother Raymond isn't dead strict.'

'Do you think he might be? He seemed nice at the *feis*.'

Liam pointed his finger. 'I think we're going to find out.'

Nora looked around and saw the Capuchin friar entering the room from a door at the back. He had flashing dark brown eyes and his grey hair was tonsured – shaved bald on the top of his head, with a fringe left all the way round – like Nora had seen in pictures of monks in her religion book. The rehearsal room had a high ceiling, there was a large crucifix on one wall and two tall windows that let in plenty of light, and Brother Raymond strode confidently to the centre of the room. He clapped his hands for attention.

'All right, boys and girls, settle down,' he said in a loud but friendly voice. 'You've all been invited here tonight – no, not simply invited – *hand-chosen*, to form a new choir. I hope you all feel honoured, just as I in turn feel honoured to have you as members.'

'You're welcome,' whispered Liam, and Nora had to suppress a laugh.

'We have lots of choirs here in Dublin,' continued Brother Raymond, 'but none of them is like ours. This will be the first mixed choir, for boys and for girls. It will be a choir where all that matters is the excellence of your singing. Not whether your family is rich or poor, not whether you're bright in school or the greatest dunce in the class! What we want here are the best singers around. Because this is going to be the best choir in Dublin!'

He paused dramatically and looked at his audience.

'What's it going to be?'

'The best choir in Dublin!' they echoed.

'I can hardly hear you,' replied Brother Raymond, exaggeratedly putting his hand to his ear, as though straining to listen. 'What's it going to be!?'

Nora looked at Liam and they both smiled, their earlier question about Brother Raymond answered. Then they joined in with everyone else and roared, 'The best choir in Dublin!'

Chapter 4

'When did you turn into a sissy, O'Meara?'

Liam knew how things worked in the schoolyard. To let a question like this go unchallenged would mean a loss of face. But to challenge too hard in return would mean a fight, which Liam didn't want either. Certainly not with Martin Connolly. He was one of the toughest boys in the class, and he had older brothers who had reputations as vicious fighters.

Liam's schoolyard was often the scene of lunchtime fights, always cheered on by boys who weren't at any risk themselves. Being fairly big for his age, Liam was rarely picked on. Now, however, Connolly had been openly insulting, and Liam saw his classmates looking for his reaction, and no doubt hoping for trouble.

'I'm no sissy,' he answered.

'Then why were you singing like a girl?'

'What?'

'My brother heard you sang *"Ave Maria"* in the Fr Mathew Hall. And that girls were singing it as well.'

'It was a *feis*. Everyone had to sing "*Ave Maria*".'

'Everyone who was a sissy.'

'What would you have done?' snapped Liam. 'Swapped "*Ave Maria*" for "The Waxie's Dargle"?'

Liam saw several of his classmates smiling at the retort. Maybe humour would get him out of this fix, he thought.

'I wouldn't be caught dead at a *feis*,' answered Connolly. 'But if I *was* singing, at least I'd sing a boy's song.'

'But it is.'

'*Ave Maria?*'

'Yeah, "*Ave Maria*" is a boy's song.'

'How is it?'

'It's a *hymn*. If it was a girl's song it would be a *her!*'

Several of the other boys laughed, and Liam could see that Martin Connolly was unsure how to respond. If he pushed for a fight now it might look like he couldn't take a joke. Liam had to take advantage of Connolly's hesitation, and he glanced past the other boy and saw his opportunity.

'Break it up, lads,' he called quietly. 'Killer's coming.'

Brother Killeen was a bull-headed teacher who was much feared, and the circle of boys quickly broke up. Liam moved away, relieved that a fight had been avoided. Just as well, he thought, that Connolly didn't know about his new friend Nora. Or about Brother Raymond's choir, that so far had nearly twice as many girls as boys. He smiled at the idea. Well, let Connolly be as thick as he liked, he was the one missing out on fun because he couldn't sing. And nothing, certainly not Connolly and his stupid brothers, would keep him from the choir. Cheered by the thought, he made his way across the yard, then the school bell rang, and he headed for his classroom, softly humming under his breath.

❋ ❋ ❋

Nora was really looking forward to this evening. Her father had booked a box for the family in the Gaiety Theatre, and soon they would be all going there for a variety show. Dressed in her best clothes, Nora sat back happily on a chair in the living room, her head tilted backwards as her mother brushed her hair. From the hall she heard the sound of the telephone ringing, then her brother David answered the call.

'Hello, who may I say is speaking, please?' she heard him say, as Mummy had trained them all to do.

'One moment, please,' he continued, then he called their father, who was reading *The Irish Times* in the drawing room.

'Hello,' she heard Daddy say, then after a moment he said, 'right' in a concerned tone. Nora sensed that something was amiss, and her suspicions were confirmed when she heard her father say, 'I'd plans for this evening, but they can be changed.'

Nora's heart sank. She loved dressing up and going into town for a show. Daddy usually got good seats and he always bought a box of chocolates. Unlike a lot of adults, he had a sweet tooth, and it had become a joke in the family that when they went to the theatre he always said, 'A treat is not a treat without a box of chocolates!' Now, however, it sounded like there might be neither chocolates nor a night out.

'Is there a problem?' asked her mother, as he came into the living room.

'I'm afraid so.'

Nora sat up, the hair brushing forgotten.

'That was the Employers' Federation,' continued her father. 'There's an emergency meeting called for tonight.'

'What's happened?' asked his wife.

'Mr Larkin is being troublesome.'

Nora saw her mother purse her lips in exasperation. 'That man should be kept behind bars.'

'He's certainly causing chaos on the docks.'

'Disgraceful.'

Nora looked at her father. 'Could you come for even some of the concert?' she asked.

'I'd like to, dear, but it's not possible.'

'But … could you not fight with Mr Larkin when you're in work tomorrow?'

'I'm afraid he doesn't confine his agitating to office hours.'

'And why is he fighting with you?' she asked

'He's not fighting with me directly. But he's fighting the shipping companies, and I have a consignment of wine held up in the docks. Sorry, Nora, I really have to attend this meeting.' He looked at her in appeal. 'You understand, don't you?'

'Yes, Daddy,' she answered, but her disappointment must have shown, for her mother patted her shoulder sympathetically.

'There'll be other nights, Nora,' she said.

'Yes,' replied Nora, then a thought struck her. 'Instead of cancelling, could the rest of us go?' she asked.

Her mother began to shake her head, but Nora got her plea in first.

'Please, Mummy, I've been so looking forward to this show.'

'I'm sorry, Nora, but I'm not venturing into town with three children, unescorted.'

'Supposing Catherine were to go with you?' her husband suggested. 'I'm sure she'd enjoy it, and we wouldn't have to disappoint Nora and the boys.'

Nora's hopes were suddenly raised. Aunt Catherine was her father's sister, and she lived in nearby Rathmines.

'I don't know, Thomas,' answered her mother, 'it's very short notice.'

'Oh please, Mummy. Let's ring and ask her!' Despite her plea, Nora could see that her mother was still doubtful. She needed something extra to sway her, and Nora racked her brain. Suddenly she had an idea. She turned back to her mother and spoke as persuasively as she could.

'Don't let Mr Larkin decide what we can do, Mummy. If we stay home, he's won.'

Her mother didn't react immediately, but Nora saw her father giving a wry smile.

'She has a point, Helen,' he said.

Her mother considered for a moment, then nodded. 'Very well, I'll telephone Catherine.'

'Thanks, Mummy,' said Nora, kissing her on the cheek. 'And rats to Mr Larkin!'

❋ ❋ ❋

'My favourite song ever?' said Liam. 'Janey, that's a hard one.'

He was sitting with Nora in the rehearsal room. Brother Raymond had been working the choir hard, but had given them a ten minute break while he slipped out to attend to some business. Nora had been telling Liam about the variety concert she had attended, and so the conversation had turned to singers and popular songs.

'Well, if I had to pick one song, it would probably be "Alexander's Ragtime Band",' continued Liam. 'It's a brilliant tune, I love the way it sort of twists and turns.'

'Yes, it's really good.'

'How about you?'

Nora looked thoughtful. 'I love "Give my Regards to Broadway". Once you start singing it, it stays in your head for days.'

'Did they do it at the variety show?'

'Yes. And they got everyone to sing along to "Oh, Oh, Antonio" and "There was I, Waiting at the Church".'

'Great.'

Nora smiled. 'Though Mummy said "Waiting at the Church" is slightly vulgar, and not what you'd expect to hear in the Gaiety!'

'I think it's a gas song,' said Liam.

'I do too.'

'So why wouldn't you expect to hear it in the Gaiety, is it really posh there?'

'You've never been?' asked Nora.

'No.'

'It's very nice, but I wouldn't call it posh.'

'You're lucky to get brought there.'

'We nearly didn't make it. Mr Larkin almost ruined the night.'

'Who's Mr Larkin?'

'Jim Larkin, the union man. Him and his blooming strikes! Daddy got called to a meeting, and we almost didn't get to the show.'

Liam was taken aback. Jim Larkin was a hero to the people that Liam knew, and this was the first time he had heard anyone speaking ill of him.

'Him and his blooming strikes?' Liam repeated. 'Do you know why he calls strikes?'

Now it was Nora's turn to look taken aback. 'I suppose …

to get more money,' she answered.

'Where do you live, Nora?'

'Leeson Park.'

'Is it a nice house, with plenty of rooms?'

'Well, yes ...'

'Lots of Larkin's men live like cattle. Whole families, ten and twelve people, in one room. Seventy or eighty people in the same house, with just one toilet out the back. My da says if you're poor and you live in Dublin, your baby is more likely to die than in most other cities in Europe.'

'Really?'

Liam could see that Nora was shocked. 'You didn't know any of this?' he said.

'No. I mean, I knew there were poor people in Dublin. But ... well, I never knew it was that bad. And what you said – you're sure that's all true?'

Liam nodded. 'My da told me.'

Nora hesitated, then spoke softly. 'I ... I'm sorry, Liam. What I said about Mr Larkin.'

He could see that she meant it and he nodded again. 'It's all right. And your da? Is he an employer?'

'Well, he's a wine importer. So I suppose he is. But he's really kind, he wouldn't be unfair.'

'Maybe not. But the way things are done is dead unfair. My da says that's the biggest challenge.'

'How do you mean?'

'He says we've got to make people see that just because things were always a certain way, that's not a good reason not to change.'

'Right. Does your father often talk to you about stuff like that?'

'Yeah, a bit. Does yours not?'

'Not really.'

'He's not always making a big thing of it,' explained Liam, in case he had made his father sound like he was always lecturing him. 'Sometimes we just chat if I'm helping him with an engine.'

'You work with him?'

'No, but I give him a hand sometimes. He's a mechanic in Gibsons, the hauliers, so some nights he'll bring home a delivery van, maybe show me how to tune an engine.'

'Brilliant.'

'Yeah, it's good.'

'I'd love to know how to tune an engine.'

Liam laughed. 'Girls don't tune engines, Nora.'

'We could if we were shown how.'

'Why would you want to do that?'

'Why do *you* want to?'

''Cause I'm interested in engines.'

She looked at him challengingly, and he felt he needed to say more. 'It's just … it's something girls don't do.'

'Because things were always a certain way, that's not a good reason not to change.' She looked him in the eye. 'Isn't that what you said?'

Liam couldn't think of a reply.

'Well?'

'I suppose it is,' he answered weakly.

Nora pointed at him and laughed. 'Got you!'

In spite of himself he had to smile back. She was cleverer than he had realised. But even though she had won this part of the argument he didn't feel that she was trying to make him appear stupid.

Just then Brother Raymond came back in. 'All right, everyone,' he called. 'Sheet music at the ready, we'll do the harmonies for *Westering Home.*'

Liam and Nora took out their music and Liam thought about what she had said about girls and engines. It was something he had never considered before – but maybe she had a point. And despite being rich, she had taken his arguments seriously when they had discussed Jim Larkin. It was an unusual friendship, but he was still glad he'd met her, and he sensed that being friends with Nora was going to be interesting.

※　※　※

'Well played, Nora. You saved a certain goal in the first half.'

'Thanks,' replied Nora to her friend Mary, as they packed away their hockey gear in the pavilion of the school's sports ground.

Out on the pitch it had been unseasonably cold for late April, but here in the changing rooms it was cosy and warm, and the nuns had arranged for soup and sandwiches to be served to the team in the dining room of the pavilion. Normally Nora took these things for granted, but since her conversation with Liam she was more aware of how lucky she was to come from a well-to-do family, who could send her to a private school.

The things he had said at their last meeting had played on her mind. The idea of babies dying because their parents were poor, and seventy to eighty people all living in one house, seemed really wrong to Nora. She had questioned her father about it last night when she found herself alone with him in the drawing room after her piano practice.

'Nicely done, Nora,' he had said. 'You've developed a good feel for Chopin.'

'Thank you.'

'All the lessons are paying off, eh?' he added with a smile.

Her private lessons, to which she had never before given a second thought, seemed like a luxury now that she knew the suffering going on in her home town. She looked at her father enquiringly.

'Daddy, why are there so many poor people in Dublin?'

He seemed slightly taken aback, but answered carefully. 'I'm afraid there are poor people in all cities, Nora.'

'But more babies die in Dublin than in other cities.'

Her father looked surprised. 'Who told you that?'

Nora hesitated. After her mother's comments at the *feis* in the Fr Mathew Hall she had made no further reference to Liam, or the fact that they were becoming good friends. *Better be careful,* she thought. 'I heard someone saying it at choir practice,' she answered. 'Is it true?'

Her father nodded his head. 'I'm sorry to say that it is.'

'But why is that allowed? And why do they make whole families live in one room?'

'They're not *made* live in one room. But they're not well educated, so they don't find well-paying employment. Which means they can't afford suitable accommodation – so they live in tenements.'

'That's not their fault though, is it?'

'No, I suppose not …'

'And why do so many babies die in Dublin?'

Her father looked uncomfortable. 'Not enough medical care, I'm afraid. And then there's the scourge of TB.'

'But isn't there anything being done to help, Daddy?'

'Well, the government tries to improve things. But every society has poverty; it's how things are.'

Because things were always a certain way, that's not a good reason not to change. Nora remembered Liam's words, but said nothing.

'I hope they're not upsetting you at this choir,' said her father.

'No,' answered Nora quickly, anxious not to provide a reason to take her from Brother Raymond's group. 'It was just something I heard,' she said, telling herself that this was only a white lie.

'The world can be harsh, Nora. We have to be kind whenever we can, and the rest of the time we must be thankful for our good fortune.'

Nora had nodded in agreement, but it hadn't seemed a satisfactory answer at the time, and thinking about it now it still didn't satisfy her.

'Hey, Nora, penny for them!'

'Sorry?' said Nora, brought back abruptly to the present by Mary, who was grinning at her.

'You're a million miles away!'

'Sorry.'

'What are you thinking?'

Nora had told Mary nothing about Liam. She wasn't quite sure why, but somehow now didn't seem the right time to explain about her new friend, and how he had made her question things. She looked at Mary. 'I'm thinking if we don't get in soon the soup will be gone! Last one's a monkey's uncle!' She turned on her heel, raced ahead of Mary, and ran out the door.

Chapter 5

A warm breeze blew in off the Liffey, carrying with it the smell of the sea. It was early June, and the sun shone brightly as Liam sat in the tiny backyard of his granny's cottage in Ringsend, happily dunking a biscuit in his mug of sweet tea. He loved Sunday mornings like this, when he and his father walked together into town and then down the quays to visit his granny.

On their way today, his father had triumphantly pointed out the premises of the big shipping companies that had just lost a major battle with Larkin's union. It had been a great victory, Da explained, with dock workers now earning five shillings for a ten-hour day. They still did gruelling work, and the men put in a sixty-hour week, but at least now they were being paid a decent rate.

Liam knew that things didn't always end so well. Only this morning they had received suspicious glances from policemen during their walk, due to Da sporting a black eye. He had taken a punch a few days previously when the DMP – the Dublin Metropolitan Police – had clashed with striking carters. Being a loyal union man, Da had supported the carters when the police had attacked them, and his wife had been horrified when he came home with a puffed-up eye. But Granny had a very different attitude.

Liam looked at her now, a small, stout woman with snow-white hair, but bright blue eyes that still had a youthful sparkle. She put down her mug of tea and looked at her son, a smile playing about her lips.

'So, this black eye,' she said. 'Tell me you gave the peelers as good as you got, Billy!'

Liam's father smiled back wryly. 'You can count on it.'

'Good for you, son. Shower of bowsies, them DMP. Mrs Milligan up in Townsend Street had her stuff destroyed by them. Broke into her room and smashed every stick of furniture.'

'Why did they do that, Granny?' asked Liam.

'Because her Christy is on strike, and himself and the lads laid into a group of scabs.'

'Scabs' were workers hired by the employers to do the job of someone who was on strike – and they were really hated. Liam looked at his grandmother and reckoned he knew where Da got his rebel blood. Then suddenly Granny's mood changed and she turned to Liam, her feistiness replaced by curiosity.

'So, anyway, tell us the latest on your choir,' she said.

'It's going great. We'll be taking a few weeks off in the

summer, then doing a big concert at the end of August.'

'Well, fair play to you! And this Brother who's in charge?'

'Brother Raymond. He's gas. He's mad about music, so if you're not serious he'll bawl you out of it. But he's good fun too. He always says music is for enjoyment.'

'So it's not just hymns?'

'Oh no. I mean, we do hymns. But we do classical pieces, and Gilbert and Sullivan, and Irish airs – all sorts.'

'Liam's even brought in a few bob from singing at weddings,' said his father. 'Didn't you, moneybags?' he added with a wink.

Liam could tell that Da was proud of him, and he smiled. 'Yeah, I got sixpence at one wedding, Granny, and nine pence at the other.'

'Me life on ye!' she said. 'And your da here was telling me it's boys *and* girls in the choir.'

'Yes.'

She looked at him playfully. 'I suppose then you've got yourself a mot already!'

Why do adults always think it's funny to ask children if they have a girlfriend or a boyfriend? Liam thought. Over the last few weeks he had gotten to know Nora better, and she was certainly his best friend in the choir. They both liked music, they both liked jokes – though Nora admitted that she wasn't all that good at actually telling them – and Liam was curious to hear about the world she lived in, that was so different to his own. So yes, she was his friend, and yes she was a girl, but she definitely wasn't a girlfriend, or as Granny called it, 'a mot'.

'Well?' persisted Granny.

'No,' he answered.

'Are you sure you haven't got some little one tucked away?' asked Granny with a laugh.

This was exactly why he had told nobody about Nora.

'Positive,' he answered.

'Oh I believe you. But thousands wouldn't!'

Liam tried for a smile. But he knew that what he told himself wasn't entirely true. There was another reason he had said nothing about Nora, and that was the fact that her family was on the other side in the battle between workers and employers. It seemed wrong that it should affect himself and Nora, and yet he sensed that his father would see it as a kind of betrayal if he knew that Liam was friends with someone whose father was a wealthy employer.

Just then they heard the deep sound of a ship's horn from the river, and his father tilted his head towards the Liffey.

'You heard that Larkin has the docks completely under his control now?'

Granny nodded approvingly. 'God bless him. That day was a long time coming.'

'It's only the start. But the bosses are furious.'

'Pity about them.'

'Absolutely,' agreed Da. 'But if we're only getting started, and they're already furious – there'll be murder by the end of the summer.'

'You think so?'

'There has to be a showdown.'

'And can you win, Billy?' asked Granny.

Da nodded. 'If we all close ranks and come down hard on scabs and traitors, then yeah, we can.'

His father's words made Liam think again about Nora, and loyalty, and betrayal, and despite the warm summer breeze, he felt a tiny chill.

✳   ✳   ✳

'Knock knock', Nora whispered to Mary as they sat together at the back of the classroom.

'Who's there?'

'Dwayne.'

'Dwayne who?'

'Dwayne the bathtub – I'm dwowning!'

Both girls giggled, though they were careful not to be seen by Miss Dillon, who now rose from her desk and turned to face the class. It was the final day of term and a hot June sun shone in through the classroom window, making the suspended dust appear to dance and shimmer in the air.

'Your attention, please, girls,' said Miss Dillon.

Nora looked up expectantly, a little surprised at how

serious her teacher appeared. Being the end of term, there was a relaxed air about the school as teachers and pupils looked forward to the summer break. Miss Dillon was a tall, thin woman whom most of the girls guessed to be in her late thirties. Normally her manner was energetic, but for some reason today she seemed subdued.

'I've news to announce, girls,' she said, and immediately Nora knew that something was wrong.

'I regret to say that today is my last day with you. I had looked forward to having you next year, but I'm afraid that's not to be. You're a wonderful group of students and it's been my pleasure to teach you.'

There was stunned silence. Looking around, Nora could see how upset the girls were to be losing a favourite teacher. Finally, Mary raised her hand and asked the question that hung in the air. 'Why won't we have you next year, Miss?'

Miss Dillon hesitated, then seemed to reach a decision. 'You're old enough to know the truth, so I'll tell you. My contract has been terminated by the school. I'm not being employed after today.'

Nora was shocked. Miss Dillon spoke again, presumably aware that some of the girls were close to tears, for now she made her tone brighter.

'On the positive side, I've acquired a post in Yorkshire,' she said. 'It's in a co-educational school in Leeds, quite progressive, by all accounts. So don't worry, I'm not going to starve.'

Her attempt at lightening the mood wasn't successful, so she abandoned what Nora had suspected was a brave face, and spoke seriously again.

'I've been told that my values are at odds with the values of the school. I've been told that you, my pupils for whom I care deeply, were with me to be taught the prescribed subjects, and the prescribed subjects only. It seems I've been raising notions in your minds, notions that upset the social order. Parents and management apparently don't want girls who are independent thinkers, and so I'm no longer to be allowed "deviate from the curriculum and create mischief", as it was put to me.'

Nora was horrified. She had assumed that nothing further had come of the discussion at home when her mother had been critical of Miss Dillon's views. Now she feared that this might not be the case. As if anticipating her concern, Miss Dillon raised a hand.

'Please, I don't want any of you to think that you're the cause of this. It's entirely natural that you would mention at home things that we discussed in school. I wouldn't want it otherwise. So none of you is in any way to blame for my situation. This is something that's probably been coming for some time. Besides, I knew when I started here that my employment was at the discretion of the Board of Management. And now they've dismissed me. So be it. But before I go there's one last thing I want to say to you all, and I'd like you to remember it.'

Nora leaned forward, hanging on the teacher's every word.

'There is nothing – *nothing* – that you are not capable of. They'll tell you that you are young ladies. They'll try to use that to disqualify you from voting, from attending university, from fulfilling your potential in all sorts of areas. *Do not allow them to succeed!* You're bright, you're capable, and you have your whole lives before you. Make something of those lives. Each one of you be the best person you can be. And let no one ever convince you that you can't do something simply because you are a woman.'

Miss Dillon paused, looked from face to face, then spoke with finality. 'There are no limits to what you can achieve. Don't allow others to limit you.' She took her satchel from the top of her desk, then nodded in farewell. 'Thank you, girls, for sharing this past year with me. It's been a privilege.'

For a moment nobody moved, then the girls began applauding. Nora had a lump in her throat, and some of the other pupils had tears in their eyes. Miss Dillon gave a small smile in recognition of the applause, which grew louder as the girls rose from their desks, until every pupil in the class stood clapping, as their teacher, struggling with her emotions, nodded once more in farewell and then left the room.

Nora felt angry that Miss Dillon had been sacked, yet inspired by her parting words. There and then she swore that she would do as her teacher had urged. More than that, she promised herself that when the opportunity arose, she would do something bold of which Miss Dillon would be proud. She wasn't sure what it might be, but she knew, instinctively, that something had changed today, and that her life wouldn't be the same again.

Chapter 6

'The three best things about summer? Janey, there's loads!' said Liam.

'But the *best* three,' persisted Nora.

'All right, let me think.' This was the kind of thing Nora was always asking. What were the nicest sweets in the world? What would you ask for if you had three wishes? What was the best piece of music ever composed? None of Liam's other friends ever asked stuff like that, but he had come to enjoy Nora's lists, and it was fun to imagine things like being a king, and deciding what your laws would be.

As he considered his answer, Liam breathed in deeply, savouring the aroma of roasting coffee. They were sitting together in Bewleys Café in Westmoreland Street where they had been brought with the other choir members for tea and buns, as a treat from Brother Raymond before the choir took a summer break. Liam had often passed Bewleys before, but this was the first time he had been inside the café. He liked the soft light from the wall-mounted gas lamps, and the hiss of steam from the tea urns. Most of all, though, he liked the cakes with their sticky yellow and pink icing and their sweet, creamy fillings. Ma and Da couldn't afford treats like this, and, like all their neighbours, they drank tea, never coffee. Still, he thought, it must be nice to be an adult with enough money to come here and order any cakes you liked, and a pot of that wonderfully-smelling coffee.

'Come on, slowcoach,' said Nora, prompting him playfully.

'All right,' said Liam, 'the three best things about summer are: no school, no school and no school.'

'Liam,' she said, laughing, 'that's cheating!'

'OK, no school, swimming in Dollymount, and ice cream cones that are just starting to melt and that have loads of that thick raspberry stuff poured over them.'

'They're all pretty good,' agreed Nora.

'So what would your three be?'

'Well, no school, I'm with you there.'

'What else?'

'Going to Torquay with my family. We go every summer. I love taking the boat to England and then the train journey to Devon; it's like an adventure.'

'I've never been to England,' said Liam. 'Is it nice?'

'Yes, very nice.'

'Have you been to London?'

'We always stay there overnight. And Daddy's brought us to see different places, like Buckingham Palace, and St Paul's Cathedral, and the Tower of London.'

'God, it's well for you,' said Liam. As soon as he said it he wished that he hadn't, because Nora looked slightly uncomfortable. Normally neither of them paid much heed to the fact that her family was much better off than Liam's. Now he sensed that she was afraid it sounded like she was boasting – although he knew she wasn't. Before he could say anything further, Nora quickly moved off the topic of London.

'And the third thing I love about summer,' she said, 'is the smell of cut grass.'

'Yeah?'

'I love the way the scent hangs in the air on a hot day. That's the smell of summer to me.'

'Right,' said Liam. He couldn't help but think that in the slums not far from his home the smell of summer was the heightened stench of unwashed bodies and pee-smelling tenement hallways, but he said nothing about this, not wanting to spoil things for Nora.

Just then Brother Raymond tapped a spoon against his cup for attention. The choir members had been allocated an alcove off the main body of the restaurant, and it fell quiet as they ceased their chatter.

'Boys and girls – singers *extraordinaire*, your attention please,' said Brother Raymond. Liam sat forward, listening with interest. He had come to really like the colourful monk. Although he could be very demanding when it came to choral work, he was never boring, and Liam liked the way that he used words like *extraordinaire* – words that other adults never used when talking to children.

'A few words of farewell before we have our short summer break,' said Brother Raymond. 'In the three months or so since we started we've made excellent progress. So, give yourselves a round of applause!'

Everybody clapped and, getting caught up in the fun of the moment, Nora even cried out, 'Bravo!'

Brother Raymond smiled. 'Steady on, Nora. It is *ourselves* we're applauding.'

Nora smiled back at him, then turned and whispered to Liam, 'But we're brilliant!'

'At any rate,' continued Brother Raymond, 'we're breaking for six weeks, reconvening on Tuesday, August the nineteenth. I hope you all enjoy the summer, but I also want you to remember that in one important respect the choir is actually like God.' He looked at them with a sparkle in his eyes. 'Anybody tell me why?'

'Because we're heavenly, Brother!' said Liam.

Brother Raymond smiled. 'A good answer, Liam – and suitably lacking in false modesty. But as Catholics you know that though you may go away on holidays, you never take a holiday from God. Likewise the choir. I want every one of you practising your singing during the summer holidays. After we get back in August, there's a charity concert at which we've been invited to sing. We'll have a limited time to rehearse for it, so I want everyone coming back in good voice and fully familiar with everything we've done so far.'

He opened his arms in appeal and looked at them. 'Can I count on you all to do that?'

'Yes!' cried the choir members.

'Good. I'll see you all next month then. Meanwhile, those who are being picked up by parents should remain here. Everyone else, safe home, and God bless.'

There was a sudden babble of conversation as those who were leaving stood and said their goodbyes.

'Are you getting the tram home?' Liam asked Nora.

'Yes. Are you?'

'No, I'll walk back up Sackville Street. But I'll come with you as far as your stop.'

'OK.'

They each said some final farewells to other choir members and thanked Brother Raymond, then Liam followed Nora out the main door of Bewleys and into Westmoreland Street. He breathed deeply one last time, absorbing the heady smell of the coffee being roasted in the front window of the café, before crossing the wide thoroughfare and heading for Nora's tram stop.

'That was really nice of Brother Raymond, treating us all like that,' said Nora.

'Yeah, he's a decent skin.'

'A decent *skin*?'

'Yeah. Have you never heard that?'

'No.'

Liam laughed. 'You don't get out enough, Nora. A "decent skin" is someone who's sound. Like, if you did me a good turn, I might say,' and now Liam slipped into a strong Dublin accent. 'Ah, you're a decent *aul' skin*, Nora!'

Nora laughed, then they arrived at her stop and she turned to face him. 'Actually you *are* a decent skin, Liam. So I got you this.'

She opened her music satchel and slipped out a small package wrapped in coloured paper.

Liam was taken aback. 'What is it?'

'A book I thought you might like.'

Liam didn't know how to respond, and seeing him hesitate, Nora spoke again.

'Just to say thanks for being my friend, and for saving me that day at the *feis*.'

'That was nothing. You didn't have to–'

'I wanted to,' said Nora simply.

She held out the book, but still Liam hesitated. One part of him was touched. But another part of him was aware that the money for the gift must have come originally from Nora's father. And however kind-hearted Nora claimed he was, her father was still on the other side in the battle being waged with Larkin's union – of which his da was such a proud member.

'Please,' said Nora. 'It's a boys' adventure book. I'd say you'd like it.'

Liam didn't want to be disloyal to his father's cause. On the other hand, Nora was his friend, and he didn't want to insult her. Looking at her outstretched arm, he wasn't sure what to do. He stood there, torn between his opposing instincts, then he suddenly made his mind up.

'Thanks, Nora,' he said, accepting the gift. 'There was no need, but thanks.'

'You're welcome.' She smiled. 'You can read it while you're eating an ice cream cone that's just melting – or even while you're swimming in Dollymount!'

Before Liam could think of a smart answer, there was a clanging sound as a tram pulled up at the stop.

'That's mine,' said Nora, indicating the vehicle and taking out her tram fare. 'So, have a good summer.'

'You too. And Nora?'

'Yes?'

'If you're at Buckingham Palace – tell the Queen I was asking for her!'

Nora laughed. 'Bye, Liam.'

'Bye.'

She boarded the tram with several other passengers, and Liam waited until the vehicle pulled off. Nora waved out the window, and he gave a final wave in return before the tram turned the corner and vanished from sight.

Liam stood there a moment, then he opened the wrapping paper and looked at the book. It was R M Ballantyne's *The Young Fur Traders*. The cover had a dramatic drawing of a boy leading a team of huskies, and Liam thought that Nora was probably right: it *was* the kind of story he would enjoy. But the important thing wasn't whether or not the book was good. The important thing was that he had accepted it. Even though he completely backed his father and Mr Larkin in their struggle, his instincts told him that taking the book from Nora was right. But it wasn't a gift he could ever show to his da.

It was complicated having a friend whose family was on the other side. And the way things were going in Dublin, it was probably going to get more complicated. But whatever happened, Liam felt that friends were friends and should stick together. The thought raised his spirits, and deciding to leave aside all worries about the future, he slipped the book into his jacket pocket, turned around and headed for home.

PART TWO

SHOWDOWN

Chapter 7

'This is the calm before the storm. When we go home things will come to a head.'

Nora listened secretly as her father sat forward in his deck-chair, talking earnestly to her mother, Aunt Catherine and Uncle Jack. They were on the beach in Devon, and Nora lay on her towel with her eyes closed, enjoying the heat of summer. Her cousins and her brothers were a little further down the strand, building an elaborate sandcastle.

Nora had come back to where the adults were sitting, to read her book for a while, then she had lain down, listening to the softly breaking waves and burrowing her toes into the hot sand. Normally her father didn't discuss work problems in front of the children, but Nora guessed that he had over-looked her presence as she lay quietly at the side of the deckchairs.

'This Larkin ruffian needs to be taken on,' said Uncle Jack.

'I couldn't agree more,' said her mother. 'Thomas has no quarrel with his staff, yet he couldn't bring in wine shipments because Mr Larkin is in dispute with the shipping companies.'

'That's simply outrageous,' said Aunt Catherine.

Nora thought of what Liam had said about poor people and the awful lives they had in Dublin. Even though she understood her father being worried over his wine shipments, it struck her that it was far more outrageous that so many poor children died in the city. She wondered if the adults ever thought of that.

'So what steps will be taken?' asked Uncle Jack.

'The employers are going to get tough,' her father answered. 'Especially on so-called *sympathetic strikes*.'

'What are they?' asked Aunt Catherine.

'It's where workers in one company down tools in support of strikers in another company.'

Uncle Jack snorted. 'Disgraceful idea.'

Nora would have loved to join in, to give the other side of the story, but she knew her mother would reprimand her if she intruded into an adult conversation. After a moment her father said that really he shouldn't have raised the topic and they should leave business for when they returned to Ireland next week.

After that the women began talking about a fund-raising bridge night for a charity on whose committee they both served. Her father and Uncle Jack drifted into a discussion of the recent application to Prime Minister Asquith to build a tunnel under the English Channel, and Nora lost interest in their conversations.

Next week they would all be returning to Dublin, and while she normally hated leaving Devon, this year she had mixed feelings. The choir would be meeting up, and she was looking forward to seeing Liam again. She would tell him about Torquay, and her visit to Buckfast Abbey, and the gypsy encampment she had seen on Bodmin Moor. She wondered how his summer was going, and wished that she could write to him, like she did to her friends Mary and Sheila. It wasn't possible of course, as he would then probably write in return, and Mummy would want to know who her correspondent was.

Her thoughts were interrupted by her aunt breaking off her chatter about the charity and speaking with concern.

'That sun is getting very hot,' she said. 'I think Sarah might need her sunhat.'

Nora heard the creaking of the deckchair as her aunt rose to get the hat, then she opened her eyes when Catherine addressed her.

'Nora, would you be good enough to bring this down to Sarah for me?'

'Of course.'

Sarah, her seven-year-old cousin, was kneeling near the water's edge, working on the moat of the sandcastle. Nora rose from the towel and took the hat. Acknowledging her aunt's thanks, she set off along the beach, the sand deliciously warm under her bare feet. In the distance she could hear a barrel organ playing 'Shine on Harvest Moon', and as she watched a seagull gliding against the bright blue sky, she was filled with a sense of happiness.

The sandcastle was a complicated piece of work that her oldest cousin, Alan, had masterminded, though it was her brothers, David and Peter, and Alan's younger sisters, Alice and Sarah, who had done most of the work. Sarah, Peter and Alice were working on a moat, and had a large bucket of sea-water that they were using to dampen sand for the moat walls.

'Here you are, Sarah,' said Nora. 'Your mum said to put this on.'

'All right,' said the younger girl, taking the hat and donning it, then immediately returning to the moat.

'Well, if it's not Nora,' remarked Alan.

He had been lying on his towel, but now he sat up, and looked at her, a smile playing about his lips.

'Nora the suffragette.'

David sniggered, and Nora felt like reaching out and pulling her brother's hair. It was so like him to try and curry favour with Alan, whom he hero-worshipped for no better reason than the fact that Alan was twelve, and so four years older.

Nora ignored her brother and turned to Alan. She kept her voice reasonable, but looked him in the eye.

'What's wrong with suffragettes?'

'Do you not know?' asked Alan

There was something unpleasant about the way he was

smiling, and Nora felt her happiness of a moment before ebbing away. Alan wasn't normally a blatant bully, but he was used to getting his own way and he had an arrogant air about him that seemed to say that he was the natural leader of any gang – and that it wouldn't be wise to cross him.

'No, I don't know,' she answered.

'They're all lunatics. Madwomen.'

'For wanting to vote?'

'Votes?' Alan gave a derisory laugh. 'They're looking for attention. And this is the only way they'll get it; most of them are too ugly to get a husband!'

David sniggered again, and Alan grinned, clearly pleased with himself.

'Who did you overhear saying that?' asked Nora.

Alan's grin faded, and Nora reckoned that her retort had hit the mark.

'You think you're smart, don't you?' he said. 'Well, you're not; those suffragettes are all as thick as a plank. And so is anyone who supports them.'

'I'm not the one who's thick.'

'Aren't you? What happened to your suffragette teacher? I bet she thought she was dead smart – till she lost her job!'

Nora felt a surge of anger. It was bad enough that Miss Dillon had been sacked, but to have her insulted by someone like Alan was infuriating. But before she could reply he gave a superior smile and spoke again.

'Catch yourself on, Nora. No woman who's a suffragette will ever get a husband.'

'Well maybe there are worse things than that.'

'Like what?'

'Like *having* a husband. Like having a husband who'd be a bully and a fool!' Nora moved forward, deliberately banging her foot against the bucket of seawater. It overturned, spilling its contents over Alan and the towel on which he was sitting.

Taken by surprise, he cried out, drenched by the cold water.

'Oh, I'm really sorry, Alan,' said Nora, then she gave him one of his own false smiles, turned on her heel and walked off down the beach.

✳   ✳   ✳

Liam's heart felt like it would burst with pride as he marched along the street to the rousing sounds of the Transport Union's Fife and Drum Band. The musicians were belting out 'O'Donnell Abu', and all along the street people were cheering and waving, savouring the novelty and excitement of Larkin's union coming to town.

Each Sunday the band marched through one of the market garden towns in north county Dublin, with Larkin himself in attendance to recruit the farm labourers into the union. Today they were in Skerries, and Liam was accompanied by his parents and sisters on a family day out. As a treat they had all travelled out on the train, dressed in their Sunday clothes and having already attended early Mass.

His four sisters had ribbons in their hair and his mother wore a straw hat with a flower in it. She had been light-hearted on the train journey, almost as though she was once again a young girl.

The band finished 'O'Donnell Abu', then the pipers launched into 'Follow Me up to Carlow'. This was an even more rousing air, and Liam felt his skin come out in goose bumps as the pipers cut loose and he and his family marched past the cheering onlookers. It was a marvellous feeling, and he wished the march through Skerries could go on forever.

By the time the musicians got to the end of the tune, the parade was reaching the outskirts of the town, and with banners flying against the clear blue August sky, the marchers turned into a field where Larkin was to address the crowd.

'All right, girls,' said Ma. 'We'll lay out the blankets and the picnic.'

While his sisters helped to spread two large blankets on the grass and to unpack the food, Liam turned to his father, who was starting to fill his pipe.

'That was brilliant, Da. Thanks for bringing us.'

His father smiled and tossed his hair. 'You're grand. And wait till you hear Big Jim addressing all these culchies. They'll be signing up in droves.'

'Here, less of the culchies, you!' said his wife in playful protest.

Liam's mother had been born in Westmeath, and so, like all country people, was called a 'culchie' by Dubliners like his father. She got her own back by calling her husband a 'jackeen'.

Ma pointed at the two blankets she had spread out on the grass. 'Onto the blankets, you lot. I don't want to see any grass stains on your good clothes.'

'Can we eat now?' asked Peg, Liam's youngest sister, when they were all safely sitting on the blankets.

'Yes, pet. But no cake till you've had your sandwiches.'

'And no talking out loud, kids, when Larkin is making his speech, all right?' said their father.

'Yes, Da,' they answered.

Liam helped himself to a ham sandwich, the loaf-bread thickly cut, the way he liked it and the ham generously spread with tangy mustard. His mother had brought rhubarb tart, his favourite desert, and he sat back happily, the summer sun warm on his upturned cheeks.

This is the life, he thought. His mind drifted to Nora, who had seemed to have such an exciting summer ahead of her. But while Nora had sailed across the Irish Sea to stay in a fancy hotel in Torquay, she hadn't marched behind a band through streets of cheering people. And she wasn't about to hear the famous Jim Larkin addressing a crowd.

He wouldn't swap with Nora for all the tea in China, as Granny would say. He wouldn't swap with *anyone*. He chewed on his sandwich, closed his eyes against the gleaming sunlight, and savoured the glorious summer day.

Chapter 8

'This is not good enough, boys and girls! Simply not good enough!' Brother Raymond pointed accusingly at the choir on this, their first night back since the summer break. 'You've two more rehearsals, then you're performing to a paying audience. And we'll be compared to the other choirs present. Are you going to let yourselves down? Well, are you?'

'No, Brother!' the choir members cried in unison.

'Good. All right, a five-minute break, then we tackle 'Oft in the Stilly Night'. And this time I want everyone in tune and paying full attention. Five minutes.'

Nora smiled to herself, aware that Brother Raymond was being a bit dramatic, when the choir was simply a little rusty after its six-week break.

Liam nudged her in the ribs. 'Come up to the landing,' he said, 'I want to show you something.'

Liam picked up the satchel in which he kept his music and led the way out of the rehearsal room. Nora followed him, intrigued.

She had come to the rehearsal early, hoping to catch up with Liam about how they had each spent the summer, but he had only just made it in time, and so they exchanged only a few details. She had been looking forward to seeing him again. The more she thought about him, the more he seemed a really pleasant contrast to her cousin Alan, who had been obnoxious for all of the second week of their stay in Torquay, after their argument about the suffragettes.

Admittedly, Liam had laughed at her when she told him she would like to learn how to tune an engine, but somehow that was different. And Liam had been genuinely sympathetic – and in fact had shared Nora's disgust – when she told him of Miss Dillon being sacked. *Why couldn't I have a cousin who was understanding and fun like Liam,* she wondered as the climbed the stairs, *instead of a stuck-up bully like Alan?*

Before she could give it any more thought, she reached the landing, and Liam turned to her and grinned.

'I didn't want the others to see,' he said. 'But I got you this.'

He reached into his satchel and handed her a stick of rock. It was bright pink in colour, at least an inch thick, and had the word 'Skerries' on the wrapper, and also running through the rock itself.

Nora hadn't been expecting anything like this, and she hesitated.

'Go on, take it,' said Liam, laughing, 'it's really good for your teeth!'

'Thanks,' she answered with a smile, but she felt a little uncomfortable.

'I ... I didn't get you anything.'

She knew that Liam didn't have much money. Having given him the present of the book when they were splitting up for the summer, she had been afraid that if she brought him a gift from Torquay as well it might have put him in an awkward position.

'Sure, you already gave me the book, so we're quits. OK?'

'OK.'

'And it was a brilliant book.'

'I'm glad you liked it.'

'So, how was Torquay?'

'Great. Well, the hotel was nice, and we did loads of swimming. But my cousins were with us.' Nora grimaced. 'Not so good.'

'That's cousins, isn't it? I've loads of them, and some are great, but some are a pain in ... the *rear end*, as Da says – when he stops himself in time!'

Nora laughed, knowing that her mother would strongly disapprove of this 'rough talk', as she would call it, but somehow Liam's humorous approach made it seem all right.

'So you went to Skerries?' she said, indicating the stick of rock.

'Just for a day. But what a day.'

'Yes?'

Liam told her all about the band, and marching though streets of crowds, and Big Jim Larkin whipping the people up into a frenzy.

It sounded incredibly exciting, far more thrilling than anything they had done in Devon, and Nora wished that she could have been there. Almost as soon as she thought it, a tiny part of her felt disloyal to her father, knowing how he regarded Larkin as an extremist. But it was only a small part of her, because even if Mr Larkin was a bit extreme, surely the dreadful conditions that he was fighting against *called* for someone extreme? And the more Nora had heard from Liam – who now spoke about things as though they were both on the same side – the more she found herself identifying with the workers.

'But do you know what was the best part of all?' asked Liam, as he came to the end of the story.

'What?'

'The trip to Skerries really paid off. For the first time ever the farm workers joined the union. And Larkin told the farmers that they couldn't pay them slave wages anymore.'

'So they paid up?'

'No, they refused. Big mistake,' said Liam with a smile. 'Because, you know what happens every August?'

'I don't know,' said Nora, eager to hear the climax of the story.

'The harvest has to be taken in. Only this time the

labourers said no. Nobody cut a blade of hay. Until yesterday – when the farmers caved in!'

'Really?'

'Da told me the men got a proper raise, and they're delighted. Isn't it great?'

'Yes, it is.'

Just then they heard Brother Raymond calling for the rehearsal to recommence.

'Hide the rock,' said Liam, 'I couldn't buy a stick for everyone in the choir!'

'OK,' said Nora, slipping the rock into her pocket.

Liam ran down the stairs. Nora followed more slowly, thinking, yet again, of how much things had changed since their first chance meeting at the *feis* – and wondering where it might all lead.

Chapter 9

'I dare say Brother Raymond means well,' said Nora's mother, 'but I'm not sure of the thinking behind this choir.'

'They are rather good, Helen,' said her father.

'Granted. But a mixed choir from quite differing backgrounds – I wonder what his objective is?'

Nora felt a stab of anxiety. She would hate to be taken out of the choir at this stage. The rehearsals on Tuesday and Thursday nights had become the highlights of her week. She loved the independence of the tram trips into town, she enjoyed the singing itself, and the choir was the only place where she was ever likely to see Liam.

She was sitting with her parents in the theatre of the Royal Academy of Music where the choir had just performed in the charity concert. They had sung well and there was an air of festivity about the night, but Nora realised that her mother had picked up on how some of the children and their parents, despite being dressed up, were from poorer backgrounds. Mummy was too well-bred to be openly offensive, and had been speaking in a low voice, but Nora was still uncomfortable. She tried to think up the best way to respond, but her father got there first.

'Perhaps as choirmaster Brother Raymond simply wants the best singers available.'

'Perhaps.'

'He does, Mummy. He said it at the first rehearsal. He wants to make us the best choir in Dublin.'

Her mother gave a small smile. 'That's rather a tall order.'

'But it's something to aim for,' said Nora. 'And I love being in the kind of choir that wants to be really good.'

'The pursuit of excellence, eh, Nora?' said her father, with a smile.

'Yes, exactly.'

The accompanist for the tenor who was next on the bill began to make her way to the piano. Glancing in her direction, Nora caught the eye of Liam, who was seated at the far side of the theatre with his parents. He winked at her, and Nora gave a discreet wave in return. She would have to be careful tonight with Liam. She could hardly tell him that her mother had warned her off the friendship because his family was poor. But neither could she appear too friendly to him, or her mother would know that she had disobeyed her.

Nora turned back to her now, anxious to settle the matter of remaining a member of the choir.

'I'd really like to stay in Brother Raymond's choir,

Mummy,' she said, then when her mother didn't immediately respond, she added, 'it's helped me as a singer, and it's definitely improved my choral work.'

'Very well, Nora, we'll see.'

Nora would have liked something more definite, but she sensed that this wasn't the time to push matters. Instead she nodded as though her mother *had* agreed, crossed her fingers for luck, and sat back and applauded as the tenor took the stage.

※　※　※

Liam was really enjoying the concert. His eldest sister, Eileen, was minding the younger girls, so tonight he had his parents to himself. It was a novelty, and even more rare to see his ma and da all dressed up and out for the night. They had sung along happily with the rest of the audience when the previous singer had performed 'Has Anybody Here Seen Kelly?' It was a slightly rowdy song that Liam loved, and he had belted it out even more exuberantly than his parents.

Aware that he had the won audience over, the singer now launched himself confidently into 'It's a Long Way to Tipperary'. Once again Ma and Da joined in enthusiastically, and when Ma caught Liam's eye during the chorus she winked at him.

'This is the life, eh, Liam?' she whispered happily, her feet tapping in time to the music.

Liam nodded. He wished that it could always be like this. It was nice to see his parents forgetting their worries for a few hours – and Liam knew that there *were* things to worry about.

He had heard his father saying that he could be locked out of his job any day now, as the Employers' Federation moved against the union. According to his da, William Martin Murphy – one of the most powerful businessmen in Dublin – was determined to break Larkin, and was sacking any worker he even suspected of being in the union. And once an employer locked a worker out, wages were stopped and the locked-out worker and his family had to try to survive on the small amount of strike pay that the union could provide.

Thinking about employers, Liam looked across the theatre at Nora's father. He was very well dressed – what Liam would definitely have thought of as 'posh' – but he also seemed pleasant. Liam had seen him smiling warmly when Nora returned to her seat after the choir had performed, and he seemed less forbidding than Nora's mother, whom Liam recognised from the *feis*.

Now that he and Nora were such good friends, Liam would have liked if his parents could have met hers. But it probably wasn't a good idea. There was too big a gap between people like them and Nora's parents. It was stupid, really, Liam thought. His family were every bit as good as the Reynolds, but he knew it would be awkward if the adults met. Besides which, he had never told his mother and father about Nora, and with a lockout looming, and her father being an employer, he wasn't going to mention her now.

Liam noticed that Nora's mother wasn't singing along, but her father was, and looking at his kind face and relaxed demeanour, Liam found it hard to think of him as the enemy. But his da would. And despite Nora's claim that he was a fair employer, maybe the people who worked for him would also think of him that way.

It would become clear pretty soon, if the war between the bosses and the workers actually broke out. Who could say what would happen then to his family, to Nora, to everyone? But tonight they weren't at war, Liam told himself. *Time enough to meet your worries when they arrive on your doorstep*, as Granny always said.

He turned away from Nora's father, looked back to the singer, who was now marching about the stage, and joined in again with 'It's a Long Way to Tipperary'.

Chapter 10

Nora hated going back to school. The thought of leaving the carefree days of summer for the routine of classes and homework always cast a gloom over the final days of August. The one thing that lightened it was the Dublin Horse Show. Nora loved the show jumping competitions where the sleekly groomed horses soared over fences that looked impossibly high, and she always enjoyed the carnival atmosphere in the Royal Dublin Society grounds in Ballsbridge. It would be thronged today with the cream of Dublin society, dressed in their finery. People would stroll the manicured walkways as the army brass band played, while horse breeders from all over Ireland would show off the country's finest mares and stallions.

Nora herself was smartly turned out in a new dress bought especially for today's visit. Peter was wearing a sailor suit, which David was teasing him about as they travelled by tram towards Ballsbridge.

'Yo ho ho and a bottle of rum,' David saluted his little brother.

'Behave, David,' said Mummy.

'I'm only playing with him.'

Mummy gave David what Nora thought of as *her look*, and David nodded and said 'OK,' then sat back sheepishly in his seat.

David always enjoyed getting Nora into trouble, so Nora couldn't help but take a little pleasure in seeing him being put in his place. Just then the tram began to slow down, and she saw her father frowning as the vehicle came to a halt.

'This isn't a scheduled stop,' he said.

Nora looked towards the front of the vehicle, sensing that something unusual was going on.

'Can you see what's happening, Thomas?' asked her mother.

Before her father could reply, the tram driver came from the front of the carriage. He was a slightly built man with a thin moustache, and he addressed the passengers in a loud voice.

'Ladies and Gentlemen, from here on you're on your own! And do you know why?' he continued, then answered his own question, 'William Martin Murphy and the Tramway Company are sacking our members wholesale. And what's our crime? Joining the union. Well, the day is over when we'll be walked on without fighting back. So this vehicle is out of service – because we're on strike!'

With that, the driver turned around and walked off,

abandoning the tram.

For a few seconds the passengers sat in shocked silence, then there was a sudden babble of raised voices.

'Outrageous behaviour!' said a whiskered elderly gentleman, whom Nora thought looked like a retired officer. 'Absolutely outrageous.'

'This is a disgrace, Thomas,' said her mother.

Her father shrugged. 'It's Larkin to a "T"'. He loves the big gesture.'

People were complaining loudly, and some started to dismount from the tram while others remained seated, as though unable to believe that Dublin Tramway drivers would really dare to walk away from their vehicles. Nora hoped that this action wouldn't scupper the family's visit to the Horse Show, and she turned to her mother.

'It's not far to the showground, Mummy. We can easily walk.'

'That's hardly the point, Nora.'

'We may as well disembark, Helen,' said her father, rising from his seat.

'Might they not send a replacement tram?'

'Knowing how Mr Larkin operates, I suspect there'll be abandoned trams all over the city.'

'That's simply appalling.'

'Nevertheless, Nora's right, we can walk to the show grounds from here. We're not going to let the Transport

Union decide how we spend our day.'

Nora was relieved that their outing wasn't going to be ruined and she rose from her seat, then stood aside to allow her mother take Peter by the hand and lead him from the tram.

Passengers were milling about on the pavement, and when Nora looked up the road, she could see another tram that had been abandoned while travelling in the opposite direction.

'What's going to happen, Thomas?' her mother asked.

'William Martin Murphy won't take this lying down.'

'What will he do?'

'Hire new men to drive his trams,' I expect, 'and smash the Transport Union. I'm afraid this is outright war.'

Even though she knew that today's events would cause hatred and conflict, Nora couldn't help but feel a thrill. Larkin had thrown down a gauntlet – and she had been present!

'Well, shall we set out?' asked her father, and Nora nodded, then started out excitedly for the Horse Show.

✳   ✳   ✳

'I have to go, Kitty,' said Da. 'I *have* to.'

'There'll be trouble at this meeting, Billy, I just know it.'

Liam stood outside the kitchen door. His sisters were skipping at a lamppost around the corner, and Liam had been playing football on the road and had come in for a drink of water. Now, however, he couldn't help but eavesdrop on his parents in the kitchen, who clearly thought they had the house to themselves.

'If there *is* trouble,' said his father, 'it won't be of our making.'

'What good is that if you're arrested? Please, Billy, I don't ask very often – skip this meeting.'

Liam stood unmoving, listening intently. His mother was right, she rarely asked his da outright not to do things, even though Liam sensed that she worried a lot about the kind of stands that he took. There was a pause, and when his father answered it was in an unusually gentle tone.

'I'm sorry, love,' he said. 'I really am. But I can't turn my back on Larkin now. There's a principle at stake.'

'And what's the principle this time, Billy?'

'Dublin belongs to the people who live here. If Jim Larkin wants to have a meeting in its main street, he's entitled to.'

'There's a warrant for his arrest. The police won't let him address the crowd.'

'That's exactly Larkin's point, Kitty. The day is over when we ask them to *let* us. We're free men and women; we're exercising the right to free speech.'

Liam felt a tingle of excitement run up his spine. Before Larkin's arrival in Dublin, the idea of defying the all-powerful employers and the police would have been unthinkable. Now it seemed like there was going to be a mass meeting in

Sackville Street, whether the authorities liked it or not.

'You could end up getting arrested.'

'They can't arrest all of us. Not if we turn up in our thousands.'

Liam thought of them all showing up to see Big Jim Larkin, and a dangerous but tempting idea lodged in his head. *This would really be worth seeing.* Supposing he pretended to be playing with his friends – and slipped into town to see what happened?

'Have we not enough to worry about?' said his mother. 'You said yourself you could be locked out next week.'

Liam had heard his da saying that four hundred employers were meeting over the coming days, and it was rumoured that they would lock out every worker who was a member of the Transport Union. If that happened, there would be twenty thousand people out of work. And the union's strike pay wouldn't go very far, not when divided among twenty thousand workers.

It wasn't as if his da's family could afford to support him, either. His brothers and sisters had children of their own to feed, and many of them were also in danger of being locked out. Liam's mother's family were small farmers in Westmeath, and Liam's granddad Crosbie, Ma's father, had never really approved of Da, and was unsympathetic to unions and workers' rights. Ma had always got on well with her sister Molly, who was married to a farmer, and who might be able to offer some support, but she lived in faraway Ballinacargy, and she also had her own children to look after.

'Maybe it won't come to all-out war,' said Da. 'Maybe the bosses will see that a lockout will hurt them as well as us. Let's keep our chins up, Kitty, OK?'

There was a pause, then Liam heard his mother saying 'right', resignedly. Not wanting to be caught listening, he gave up on his drink of water and quickly tip-toed back across the front room and out the open hall door.

The late August sky was turning golden as the sun started to set, but Liam barely noticed. His mind was on tomorrow and the showdown that was looming between the police and Larkin. *He had to be there to see it.* He would be in all sorts of trouble if he was caught, but he didn't care. His mind suddenly made up, he closed over the hall door, headed down the road and returned to his game of football.

Chapter 11

Nora sensed that something was wrong as soon as she stepped into the rehearsal room. Several of the other choir members looked at her, their attitude suggesting that there was drama in the air. She crossed to them quickly, but before she could ask what was up, Maurice Fitzgerald spoke.

'Isn't it terrible about Liam?'

Nora felt an iciness in her chest. She realised that as Liam's closest friend in the choir she was assumed to know what had happened. She looked at Maurice, finding it hard to get the words out. 'What ... what happened him?'

'He was in the riot in Sackville Street. He got hit on the head with a baton.'

Nora's mouth went dry and she felt her heart thumping. She had heard about the riot two days previously when Mr Larkin had been arrested at the Imperial Hotel, and she had worried that Liam's father might have been among the many who had been injured. It hadn't occurred to her that Liam himself would have been allowed to attend the meeting.

'Is he … is he all right?' she asked, afraid of what the answer might be.

'We don't know,' answered Maurice. 'He's still in hospital.'

'Who told you?'

'Brother Raymond was talking to Liam's mother.'

Nora looked across the room to where Brother Raymond was handing out sheet music for a new piece they were planning to rehearse. She quickly crossed to him and tipped his arm.

'Excuse me, Brother,' she said.

'Nora.'

'I just heard about Liam. Is he all right?'

Brother Raymond grimaced, his dark eyes concerned-looking. 'He got a very bad knock, Nora. Very bad.'

'He's not …?' Nora wasn't able to put her worst fears into words.

Brother Raymond clearly sensed her fear, because he touched her arm and looked at her kindly.

'He's not in danger, Nora.'

'Thank God.'

'Yes indeed. I think Our Saviour must have been looking out for him. If you like, I can bring him a message for you; I'll be visiting him later.'

'Where is he, Brother?'

'Temple Street Children's Hospital.'

When she thought about it afterwards, Nora couldn't

remember actually making a decision, but immediately after the friar gave her the information she found herself heading for the door.

'Thank you, Brother,' she cried over her shoulder.

'Nora! Nora, come back!'

But there was only one place she wanted to be. Clutching her music satchel under her arm, Nora ran out the door and made for the hospital.

She knew its location from when her friend Mary had had her tonsils removed. She cut through squalid back streets that she would normally have avoided. The journey was a blur of smelly alleyways, barking dogs, ragged children and dung-filled roadways, but Nora felt a pressing need to see for herself that Liam was all right.

She entered the hospital's main door and looked about. The woman on the reception desk appeared forbidding, and Nora paused a moment. She breathed deeply, catching her breath and deciding how to approach the receptionist. She wasn't sure what visiting hours were or whether a child on her own would be allowed to see a patient. On the other hand, she was well-dressed and well-spoken, and that tended to get you taken seriously. Without waiting any further she crossed to the desk and spoke confidently.

'Hello, I'm looking for Liam O'Meara, please.'

The woman looked at her appraisingly, and Nora added, 'I'm his sister, Nora.'

The receptionist hesitated, looked at Nora a moment longer, then seemed to make up her mind. She consulted a ledger on her desk. 'St Mary's ward. First floor.'

'Thank you,' said Nora, then she quickly turned away and made for the stairs. She ascended to the first floor, then followed the signs for St Mary's. There was a strong smell of disinfectant and floor polish, and as Nora glanced into other wards she realised that there weren't many visitors about. Perhaps visiting hours hadn't officially begun, she thought, and only close family members were being allowed in. *Just as well I claimed to be Liam's sister.*

She came to the end of the corridor and turned left into St Mary's ward. It was a long room with a high ceiling. Nora looked about, half afraid of what she might see, then she spotted Liam. He was in the last bed on the left. His head was heavily bandaged, but, other than that, he looked all right, and Nora was relieved that he wasn't unconscious or hooked up to the kind of tubes that she had seen attached to sick children as she passed the other wards. Instead Liam was propped up in bed and was reading a book.

He hadn't seen her, and suddenly Nora felt a little shy. Her mother had taught her that it wasn't courteous to call on people unexpectedly, but surely this was a special case? She hung back for another second or two, then she decided she was being silly and approached Liam's bed.

'Hello, Liam,' she said.

He looked up in surprise. 'Nora!'

'How are you feeling?'

'My head's sore, but I'm OK. How did you get in?'

'I ... I told them I was your sister. I hope you don't mind.'

Liam laughed, and Nora's spirits lifted at the sound.

'Fair play to you,' he said. 'They've all these stupid rules about who can visit, and how long you can stay.'

'I don't want to tire you ...'

'You're grand. It's great to see you.'

'You too,' said Nora, as she sat down in the chair that was beside the bed. 'So', she said, looking at him seriously, 'what did the doctors say?'

'I have to leave the stitches in for another while. But tonight could be my last night in hospital. If everything is all right they'll let me go home tomorrow.'

'That's really good.'

'Yeah. How did you know I was here?'

'I found out a few minutes ago, at choir practice.'

'And you skipped practice?'

'Yes.'

'I hope you don't get into trouble with Brother Raymond.'

'It should be OK. I'll go back for the second part of the rehearsal.'

'Right.' He looked at her, his expression serious. 'Thanks for coming, Nora.'

'I had to know you were all right. So, what happened?'

Liam shrugged and Nora realised that he had probably told this story innumerable times. 'I sneaked into town to see the meeting,' he said. 'But the police went mad; they just attacked anyone they saw. I got a baton on the head, and next thing I remember I was in here.'

'That's terrible. Was it really scary?'

Liam hesitated, then nodded. 'Yeah, it was.'

'The police should be ashamed.'

'I know. Sackville Street was awful, there were bodies everywhere. Da said there were two killed and dozens taken to hospital.'

'And what did he say about you being there? Are you in huge trouble?'

'That's the thing,' said Liam. 'I thought Ma and Da would kill me. But I was knocked out, and they were so relieved when I came to that they didn't really give out at all.'

'Right,' said Nora. She couldn't help but wonder if her parents would react like that if she had done something as outrageous as Liam had.

'I'd nearly prefer if they were angry,' said Liam. 'Like … I feel bad for worrying them so much, with all that's going on.'

'I know what you mean.'

'I don't think so, Nora,' said Liam gently. 'You see, there's a good chance that Da will be out of a job tomorrow. The employers are having a meeting, and everyone says they're going to lock out the men.'

Nora felt guilty, fearing that her father might be involved with this as a member of the Employers' Federation. 'I'm really sorry,' she said.

'We'll manage somehow. That's what Da says anyway.'

'Well, I'm sure he knows what he's talking about,' said Nora as encouragingly as she could. But, she wondered, did *her* parents know what they were talking about? Daddy claimed he had some sympathy with the workers, but that the unions wanted too much power; her mother said that Mr Larkin was a criminal agitator. But who had too much power, she thought, when the police could baton the people of Dublin and put a ten-year-old boy in hospital? She didn't say any of this to Liam, still feeling a kind of loyalty to her parents. But things were coming to a head. And as she sat by her friend's hospital bed she knew that sooner, rather than later, she was going to have to choose which side she was on.

Chapter 12

'Please, Mr O, see it as a friendly warning.'

'Thanks very much, Mrs Riordan,' Liam heard his mother respond. 'It's good of you to look out for us.'

He sat forward in his bed, straining not to miss any of the exchange taking place in the front room between his parents and Mrs Riordan, a neighbour who lived round the corner.

Liam had been discharged from hospital the previous day. His head wound was healing well and the doctors said that next week he should be able to return to school and have the stitches removed – neither of which Liam was looking forward to. Now, though, he was hanging on every word, listening through the slightly ajar bedroom door as Mrs Riordan passed on a message from her nephew, a policeman in the DMP.

'Mick is a good lad, Mr O,' she said, 'he's only tipping you the word for your own good.'

Once again, it wasn't his father who acknowledged their neighbour. 'We know that, Mrs Riordan,' said his mother. 'Don't we, Billy?'

'Yes,' said his father, slightly curtly. 'Thank you.'

'He's not happy with some of the things the DMP have had to do,' continued Mrs Riordan.

'*Had* to do?' his father challenged. 'They didn't have to baton-charge men, women and children in Sackville Street? Our Liam is lucky to be alive.'

Liam normally didn't like to hear his da getting angry, but there was something pleasing about hearing him getting agitated on his behalf.

'Sure isn't that what I'm saying, Mr O?' said Mrs Riordan. 'Mick is a decent lad; he'd be against that stuff. So when he saw your name and address on a list at the station, he knew you must be a neighbour – and he tipped me off.'

'They've funny priorities, the DMP,' Liam's father said. 'Keeping working men like me under observation, when they could be going after criminals.'

'I know. But sure that's the way, in the times that are in it,' said Mrs Riordan. 'Anyway, I better get home; I've to put on a herring for Tommy's tea.'

'I'll see you out,' Liam's mother said. 'And thanks again.'

'Mind yourself, Mr O.'

'Mrs Riordan.'

Liam heard the hall door being opened and then closed as their gossipy neighbour left. He could understand his da's irritation – he had been locked out of his job only the previous day, along with thousands of other workers across the city – and now he was being spied on as well.

'She means well,' said his mother on her return.

'I know she does, Kitty. But that doesn't mean she's not being used.'

'How do you mean?'

'Maybe her nephew Mick *isn't* doing us a favour. Maybe it's a DMP tactic. Frighten individuals into thinking the police are watching them.'

'Do you really think that's what they're up to?' his wife asked.

'It's war, Kitty. There's twenty thousand men affected by the lockout. And next week the Master Builders are threatening to lock out three thousand labourers if they don't sign a pledge not to join the union. They'd use any tactics.'

'Either way, Billy, be careful. We don't want the police on us.'

'Don't worry.'

'I mean it. If you were put in jail, I don't know what we'd do.'

'I won't be jailed. It'll be fine, love, don't fret. Stick on the kettle there, will you?'

Liam heard his mother running the tap and he thought over what he had heard. It was OK for his father to say 'don't worry'. But it *was* worrying. If the authorities could keep Jim Larkin in jail despite all sorts of protest, then they could certainly lock up someone less well known, like Da. Liam prayed that that wouldn't be the case. Because if it was, what would happen the family then?

Chapter 13

Nora was playing badly, her attention poor as she ploughed her way through Chopin's 'Nocturne in E flat'. Mr Gannon, her piano teacher, sighed heavily as she stumbled through a sequence that she normally played fluently. He was an elderly, sad-eyed man who came to their drawing room every week to give Nora a lesson, and he looked at her now in apparent sorrow.

'Concentration, Miss Reynolds, concentration, please.'

'Sorry,' answered Nora. She wished that instead of playing Chopin and Beethoven she could perform catchy pieces like 'Won't You Come Home, Bill Bailey?' or the new song that was all the rage, 'You Made Me Love You', but both Mr Gannon and her mother would be horrified if she even suggested it.

In truth, the problem today wasn't the music, it was that Nora was distracted by all that was happening. Mr Larkin had just been released from prison, and Liam had told her that he had triumphantly addressed a huge gathering outside Liberty Hall. Despite the inconvenience that had been caused by abandoning the trams during Horse Show week, there was a lot of public sympathy for the locked-out workers, partly because of the actions of the police in batoning so many law-abiding citizens during the recent trouble in Sackville Street.

Nora was looking forward to choir practice tomorrow night, to hear the latest developments from Liam, whose father seemed to be in the thick of all the action. Now, though, she finally reached the end of the Chopin piece, and Mr Gannon looked at his fob-watch, then nodded. 'Enough for today, I think. For next week I'd like you to practise "*Für Elise*", please.'

'I will,' said Nora.

'And the Chopin piece – please, Miss Reynolds, some application during the week, yes?'

'I will, I *really* will,' promised Nora.

She smiled at Mr Gannon as he stood, preparing to leave, and he nodded in return.

'Very well then,' he said.

Nora felt affection for the softly-spoken piano teacher, and she was grateful that even when she played badly, like today, he never reported the fact to her mother. She waved to Mr Gannon as he left, and the idea of being reported made her think of Brother Raymond.

Following her hasty exit to visit Liam in the hospital, she had returned for the second half of the rehearsal and apolo-gised for leaving without permission. Brother Raymond seemed to understand her anxiety over Liam. Nora had pleaded with him not to inform her mother of what she had done, knowing it would be the end of her membership of the choir if he did. Perhaps Brother Raymond knew it too, for he had chided her gently but then agreed that just this once he would let the matter rest.

Nora left the music room now, making for her bedroom and looking forward to eating the bar of chocolate that was her weekly treat after her lesson. She entered the hallway and from the opened door of the drawing room heard her mother speaking angrily.

'Mr Dickens is right, Thomas, the law is simply an ass!'

Nora paused, curious to discover what had made her mother so cross.

'Quite,' answered her father.

'What is the point in locking up an agitator like Larkin only to free him in less than two weeks?'

'Well, he's not actually free, dear. He's released on bail, pending trial.'

'Stuff and nonsense, Thomas, he should still be in prison.'

'Perhaps, but–'

'And travelling to England to address mobs of workers? Raising funds there for so-called strike pay? It's outrageous, the law shouldn't allow it!'

Nora was partly amused to hear her normally controlled mother so fired-up, but part of her was irritated too. Why did Mummy always expect the law to support people who were already rich and in charge of everything? As far as Nora could see, the law usually worked against suffragettes, or unions, or any of the people trying to make things better. So if just this once the law was an ass for releasing Mr Larkin, then Nora was in favour of asses!

The notion brought a smile to her lips, and she forgot the irritation she had felt against her mother. Instead she turned away from the drawing room door and took the stairs two at a time, eager to reach her bedroom and the waiting bar of chocolate.

Liam walked excitedly along the docks with his father at his side. This was an area he knew well from their trips to visit Granny in Ringsend, but today they had a different reason for walking down the quayside. Lots of other people were converging on the banks of the Liffey, and there was an air of drama as the assembling crowd looked expectantly down the river, everyone wanting to be the first to spot the ship that was due in port at any minute.

Liam could hardly believe his luck the previous night when Da had agreed to him coming along today, especially when his mother argued that there might be trouble with the police. Da however had claimed that there should be no trouble – they weren't picketing, or striking or clashing with blacklegs – today they were welcoming a ship to the port, and it was an historic event that he felt Liam ought to see. For the ship that the hundreds of onlookers were awaiting was the *Hare*, and it carried a cargo of food for the hungry, locked-out workers of Dublin.

Jim Larkin had been campaigning vigorously in England, and with the funds supplied by sympathetic workers there he had purchased the food and commissioned the *Hare* to carry it across the Irish Sea and up the Liffey into the heart of the city. Da had explained that Larkin's union was badly stretched and could only afford limited strike pay, but the idea of successfully appealing to mass meetings of British trade unionists for support and then dramatically shipping in food for the hungry workers and their families was classic Larkin.

Even though Liam didn't know all the details of the dispute between the Employers' Federation and the union, he could understand perfectly how Larkin had become a hero to the struggling people of Dublin, and today Liam was proud that his father was one of Larkin's supporters.

'How will they give out the food, Da?' he asked.

'Once the *Hare* docks, Larkin himself will supervise the unloading, then we'll take all the food to Liberty Hall and parcel it up.'

As Liberty Hall was the union headquarters, that made sense to Liam, but he couldn't imagine how they would divide the food fairly when there were over twenty thousand workers locked out. So far, his own family had been surviving on Da's strike pay and the money Ma made as a part-time dressmaker, but other families were already going hungry.

'How will they find a fair way of sharing the food, Da?' he asked.

'Each worker gets a docket with his strike pay. They produce it at Liberty Hall and get a food parcel. What's in it is decided by the number of people in their family.'

That sounded fair to Liam, but then a worrying thought struck him.

'What happens if the police take the food?'

'I'd like to see them try!'

Liam thought of how the police had behaved in Sackville Street, and even though they were present on the docks today in far smaller numbers he wasn't as confident as his father.

'You don't think they might?' he said.

'Don't worry, son. I wouldn't have brought you if there was going to be trouble. Having your head split once was enough, what?' he added with a grin.

'I wasn't worried about myself, Da, but it would be awful if they took any of the food.'

'If they try taking so much as a loaf of bread it'll be the sorriest day of their lives,' his father answered with conviction. 'But it won't happen. The DMP are still a shower of bowsies and bullies, but since we started defending ourselves they've had to change their tune.'

Liam had heard how groups of men had begun to arm themselves with sledge hammer handles to protect their colleagues from police attack.

'They used to attack us without batting an eyelid, now they have to think twice. Here, I'll show you,' his father added.

Liam couldn't believe it when his father stopped in front of a nearby policeman and looked at him cheekily. The DMP man was about six feet tall and heavily built and had been looking with suspicion at the passing workers as they made their way along the quays. Now he locked eyes with Da, but before the man could say anything, Da spoke up.

'Not laying into so many strikers now, are you?' he asked the policeman. 'Must be awful to have your fun spoiled by men who'll stand up to you.'

Liam saw the anger flare in the man's eyes, and for a moment he thought he was going to reach for his baton. But he seemed to check himself, his eyes blazing.

'If you know what's good for you, slum-rat, you'll shut your trap,' said the DMP man.

Da stood his ground.

'And if you know what's good for *you*, pal, you'll change your ways, and steer clear of Dublin men walking their own streets.'

Liam swallowed hard, fearing the policeman might punch Da, or try to arrest him, then suddenly a cheer went up along the quayside.

'The *Hare*! It's the *Hare*!'

All at once everyone seemed to be running forward, and Liam and his father were swept along with the crowd, leaving the DMP man behind. Liam was relieved that his father hadn't been arrested, and thrilled that he had gotten away with standing up to, and – if the truth were told – taunting a policeman.

The cheers became louder and, looking down the river, Liam saw the *Hare*, laden with supplies, steaming proudly up the Liffey. Liam thought it was one of the best sights he had ever seen. Da looked at him and smiled, then they both turned back towards the approaching ship and cheered until they were hoarse.

Chapter 14

Nora jumped from the tram before it came to a halt, lightly hitting the pavement at a run. It was a mildly daredevil act that she really enjoyed, all the more so as it was the kind of thing she could never do when travelling with her parents. She made her way along Burgh Quay, feeling excited over what she was about to do next, but also a little anxious. If her parents objected to her jumping from a moving tram, they would have been horrified at the thought of her going to meet Liam at Liberty Hall, the headquarters of Mr Larkin's union.

She had told her mother that the choir was singing at two weddings today, and she still felt slightly guilty over deceiving her. But Nora felt she had no choice, it was the only way she could meet the challenge that Liam had set her. In fairness to him, he hadn't intended to test her, but when she had praised him at rehearsals for helping to distribute the food delivered by the *Hare*, he had queried if she really meant it.

'Of course I mean it,' Nora had said.

'Why don't you give us a hand then?'

Nora had been taken aback, but Liam didn't seem to think it was an unusual request. 'There's another ship coming this week with more food. We'll be delivering some of it to people who are too old or sick to collect it themselves. If you want to help, you can.'

Norah had hesitated, but only briefly. 'All right, I'll help.'

'Are you sure?'

'Yes, certain.'

'Thanks, Nora, you're dead sound.'

Liam smiled, and Nora had felt good, both at the compliment and at doing what felt like the right thing.

Now, as she made her way to Liberty Hall, she still thought it was right to help, but she was nervous. She had never been anywhere like the union hall before. She wasn't sure what the people there would be like, and how they might respond to her, dressed as she was in expensive clothes and hand-made shoes.

Before she had time to worry any further she reached the entrance and stopped. The union headquarters was really busy, with men whom her mother would have described as *rough* bustling in and out the doors. There were women going in and out too, most of them wearing shawls, and many of them with under-nourished children. Nora watched for a moment, then she steeled herself and followed a woman with three gaunt-looking little girls who passed through the entrance door.

The woman seemed to know where she was going, and Nora followed her along a corridor that opened into what she assumed was the main assembly area. It was noisy and crowded. Along one wall people were making up food parcels, while at the back of the room meals were being served from a big kitchen. The rest of the room was taken up with those who were queuing for the food parcels that were already made up.

There was so much going on that nobody paid any particular attention to Nora. Despite the fact that anyone queuing here was obviously in need, and that it was now four weeks into the lock-out, there was a good deal of banter among them. Nora was surprised. *How cheerful would I be if there was no money coming in to my family for that long?* she wondered.

'There you are!' said Liam, suddenly appearing by Nora's side. 'So you got out OK?'

'Yes, Mummy thinks I'm singing at a wedding.'

'Well, you can give us a few bars of "*Ave Maria*" if you like.'

'Maybe I'll just help with the parcels,' Nora said, with a grin.

'Grand,' Liam responded. 'Come on, I'll show you the drill.'

Nora was impressed at how Liam seemed to be completely in his element here. He led the way to where a stack of labelled parcels had been placed on a table in a corner.

'These are all addressed for delivery. There's two packages

here for around Dorset Street. Do you want to carry one and I'll take the other?'

'Fine,' said Nora. She read the name on the first package. 'Who's Mrs Perkins?' she asked.

'She's an old woman who's been trying to get by on her own since her son died.'

'Oh. What happened to him?'

'He had an accident in Naughton's Mills. Got crushed when a beam collapsed. He was a union man so they have to look after the mother.'

'Right,' said Nora, conscious that there was a world of which she had barely been aware, where workers got killed and their dependents risked starvation. 'And the other one?'

'Jem Whelan. He used to be a docker till he injured his back. He can't walk properly now, so we'll bring the parcel up to him.'

'OK,' answered Nora, impressed by the way the union organisers, despite being short of funds, seemed to look out for the needy.

Liam picked up one of the parcels. 'You can take this one,' he said, placing it in her arms. 'Not too heavy, is it?'

Nora thought it *was* fairly heavy but she shook her head. She thought of how Cook served her family with fine food every day, whereas the people getting these parcels possibly had no idea where their next meal was coming from. 'It's fine,' she answered, then Liam hoisted the second parcel.

'All those women, Liam,' Nora said, indicating the busy group serving in the kitchen. 'Who are they?

'A lot of them are in the Irish Women Workers' Union.'

'Really?' said Nora, who didn't know that a union for women existed.

'See the woman in the red top over there? She's Delia Larkin, Jim Larkin's sister. She helped start the women's union. She's one of the main people running all this,' said Liam, indicating the busy kitchen and the food parcels.

Nora was impressed that not alone were suffragettes seeking votes for women at the parliament in Westminster, but here in Ireland women were also taking it on themselves to change things.

'That's great,' she said.

'Yeah, she's sound,' said Liam. 'The other women here are mostly wives of members. As well as helping out, it means they get to have at least one meal a day.'

'One meal?'

'A lot of them were going without their share of food so their kids wouldn't go hungry.'

Nora was shocked. She hadn't known what she would encounter in Liberty Hall, but she hadn't expected to find that women were starving themselves to feed their children.

'I'm just going to deliver these two, Mr Brennan,' called Liam to a man who was busily sorting more parcels.

'Work away, son,' he called distractedly, 'work away.'

'Right, your first delivery,' said Liam with a smile, then he led the way out of Liberty Hall and they started walking up Gardiner Street.

They chatted about the choir as they carried the precious foodstuffs, occasionally setting down the parcels to give their arms a rest. They walked through a part of Dublin that wasn't familiar to Nora, and she was struck by how different these streets were to the leafy roads around her own home in Leeson Park. They were lined on either side by tall, dilapidated tenement houses, their hall doors wide open and their windows frequently broken, with tattered wisps of net curtains hanging out.

Judging by the number of bedraggled children playing on the stone steps and swinging from ropes tied to the lampposts, she reckoned there must be lots of large families living in each house. She pulled her warm coat around her and tried not to think of how cold it must be in those rooms, with their broken windows, and probably no money to buy coal for fires.

They made their way towards Dorset Street, then Liam turned down a narrow, gloomy laneway to get to Mrs Perkins' house. On one side of the laneway there was the high wall of a factory, and on the opposite side was a terrace of ramshackle tenements. Nora could hear a baby screaming through the open door of one of the houses. She hoped against hope that Mrs Perkins didn't live in one of these buildings, and her heart sank when Liam indicated that the second last house was their destination.

They climbed the granite steps.

'Watch where you walk,' said Liam as they entered the darkened hallway and made for the stairs.

'OK,' said Nora, avoiding a wrecked-looking pram that lay against the wall, and fighting back her revulsion at the smell of pee coming from the rear of the hallway.

They climbed the rickety stairs, and while Nora hadn't expected the stairway to be carpeted, she was taken aback to find that in places there wasn't even a banister.

Liam must have noticed her looking at gaps. 'People burn the banisters when they've nothing else,' he said in explanation.

'Right,' answered Nora, trying not to look too shocked.

When they reached the second floor Liam checked the address on the parcel, then he crossed the landing and knocked on a heavy door covered in peeling cream paint.

'Union delivery, Mrs Perkins,' he called out. 'Parcel from Liberty Hall.'

The door was opened almost immediately, as if Mrs Perkins had been expecting the knock, and a small, wizened woman with wiry grey hair and wearing a heavy black shawl stood before them. She could have been any age from about sixty to eighty, Nora reckoned, but though her skin was wrinkled, her dark brown eyes were alert, and she smiled a gap-toothed smile.

'You're as welcome as the flowers in May!' she said brightly. 'Come in, come in'.

Nora and Liam entered a high ceilinged-room that had a bed in one corner, a large fireplace with no fire in the grate, and a battered-looking table and chairs near to a window that overlooked the backyard. The room smelt damp and musty and the only form of decoration was a couple of religious pictures – a portrait of the Sacred Heart over the fireplace and a picture of the Virgin Mary that hung over the bed.

'I'll just leave this on the table,' said Liam, setting down the food parcel. 'There's milk, tea, sugar, and bread. Even a bit of corned beef.'

'The blessings of God on you, son!' said Mrs Perkins, holding Liam by the arm.

'You're grand.'

'God and his Holy Mother will reward the two of yis,' insisted the old woman.

Nora smiled politely. 'Glad to help.'

Mrs Perkins went to the table and quickly opened the parcel, taking out a packet of tea. 'Let me make a cuppa, it'll warm yis up.'

'Thanks all the same,' said Liam, 'but there's no need.'

'I'm making one for myself, anyway. Mrs Murray next door's after bringing in a pot of boiling water. She's a saint, that woman, and her with seven chiselers of her own to look after. Sit down there now and have a cuppa with me.'

Nora saw Liam hesitate briefly, then he nodded and sat down. 'Fair enough. No sugar, thanks, and not too strong, please.'

Nora suspected that Liam didn't really want the tea, but knew that it would make the old lady happy.

'You'll have some too, won't you, love?' said Mrs Perkins now, turning to Nora and placing three chipped cups on the table.

A girl in school had told Nora that millions of germs could live in the crack in a tea cup, and Nora's first instinct was to refuse, but the hopeful look in Mrs Perkins's eyes stopped her.

'Yes, thank you,' she said, 'that would be lovely.'

❋   ❋   ❋

'First time in a tenement house?' Liam asked, as they made their way up Dorset Street to deliver the second parcel.

Nora felt uncomfortable. 'Was it that obvious?'

'No. You were really nice to Mrs Perkins.'

'But you knew I was ...' Nora wasn't sure how to put it into words, for fear of sounding offensive.

'A bit shocked?'

'Well ... yes.'

'*I* knew it,' said Liam, 'but she wouldn't have. You live in a fancy neighbourhood, Nora. No one could blame you for being shocked. It's good that you're helping at all, I'm really grateful.'

'Thanks, Liam,' she answered, touched by his words. 'We're so lucky, aren't we? Compared to some people?'

'Yeah. But don't let slip at home what you were doing.'

'Don't worry, I'll be careful,' she said, then she turned to him. 'What about your father? I thought I might see him in Liberty Hall today.'

Liam looked away, and Nora sensed at once that he was uncomfortable.

'He's over in Terenure. They're picketing a print works.'

Nora wondered if that was why Liam had invited her today, because his father wouldn't be there. She stopped and faced him. 'He doesn't know we're friends – that I even exist, does he?' she asked softly.

Liam shook his head a little sheepishly. 'No', he answered.

Even though they were good friends, this was something they had never discussed before. Somehow, though, the words had come out today, and now that they had, Nora was glad, even though Liam looked a little awkward.

'It's OK, Liam,' she said gently. 'I haven't told Mummy about you, for the same reason you haven't told your dad about me.'

'It's not that I'm ashamed of you as a friend, Nora, it's just …'

'I know. There'd be too much trouble with our parents.'

'Yeah.'

'We can just keep it this way,' said Nora. 'Keep it our secret. Can't we?'

'Yes', said Liam, 'of course.' Now that the matter had been resolved, he perked up again. 'It's like my granny says, "What they don't know won't hurt them!"'

'Exactly. So, secret friends then. Deal?'

Liam grinned, lowered his parcel to the ground, then held out his hand and shook Nora's. 'Deal!'

❋　❋　❋

Liam collided with Martin Connolly as they both went for the ball. Liam won the ball, and Martin lost his balance and fell. Swivelling quickly, Liam took a shot at the makeshift goal, marked by two sweaters on the concrete schoolyard, but the goalie was agile and saved. Disappointed, Liam turned away and saw Connolly rising a little shakily. He remembered how the other boy had almost goaded him into a fight over singing in the *feis* some time back, but there was nothing to be gained by antagonising the toughest boy in the class, and he reached out and offered him a hand up.

In fairness to Connolly, although he was a rough player, he never complained when on the receiving end of a hard tackle himself, and he accepted Liam's gesture and rose to his feet.

Liam was a little taken aback at how light Connolly had felt. But lots of families were struggling to find enough to eat now that the lockout was in its sixth week, and the Connollys had been poor to begin with. Still, it was disturbing that someone as seemingly indestructible as Martin Connolly should be getting thin from lack of food.

The prospect of the lockout ending soon wasn't good either. Liam had heard his father saying that the employers had rejected the government's attempt to reach some kind of settlement. An 'all-out war, fought to the bitter end' was what his da said they could expect, and Liam feared that the coming winter was going to be really tough.

He tried to put aside his worries and turned back to the game, running towards the opposition goal and calling for the ball. But the boy who had the ball shot at goal himself, and Liam was just about to complain to him when he heard Brother Killeen calling his name.

Liam felt an immediate stab of unease. Being summoned by 'Killer' Killeen rarely meant good news, but Liam knew better than to delay, so he quickly left the football game and crossed the yard to where he could see Brother Killeen at the gate.

To Liam's amazement, his mother was standing behind the bull-like figure of Killeen. The brother spoke with unusual gentleness. 'Your mother needs to speak to you, Liam.'

Being called by his Christian name only confirmed Liam's dread that something bad had happened, and when he saw Ma's face his fears grew worse.

'I'll leave you to it, Mrs O'Meara,' said Killeen, discreetly departing.

'What's happened?' asked Liam. 'Is it Da?'

His mother nodded, and Liam looked at her, afraid to ask the next question. He knew that two men had been beaten to death during the rioting. It would be unbearable if the same thing had happened to his da, but he was such a hot-head that he might easily have gotten himself into trouble.

'Is he ... is he ...'

'He's OK, Liam. But I need you to come home to mind the girls. I have to go to your da.'

'Why? What's happened?' demanded Liam, deeply worried by the way his mother was trying to stop her voice from quivering.

'He ... he's been arrested. The police are holding him down at the station – and he's going to be sent to prison.'

Liam swallowed hard. Part of him knew this had always been a possibility, but now that his father had actually been taken away it felt like his world had been turned upside down. His mother reached out for him, but he didn't want to be seen hugging her in the schoolyard, and instead he took her hand and quickly squeezed it. Then, holding back his tears, he walked wordlessly beside her as they made for home.

✳   ✳   ✳

'What are we going to come up with for this fancy dress?' Mary asked as the two school friends walked down the corridor towards their classroom.

'I had a brainwave last night,' answered Nora. 'Supposing we get *sombreros* and go as two Mexican girls?'

The girls had been invited to a party in Rathmines that was being hosted by the family of one of their school friends, Sheila Mulcahy. Sheila's father was the senior engineer in the Irish branch of an international engineering company involved in the building of the Panama Canal. Although the canal wouldn't be formally opened until the following year, last Friday had been a great day for the company. The newspapers had all reported that President Wilson had pressed a button on his desk in the White House, causing a charge to be detonated four thousand miles away in Panama, to remove the final obstacle to the waterway that would link the Pacific and Atlantic oceans. Mr Mulcahy claimed that the canal was the greatest piece of engineering so far in the twentieth century, and had decided to celebrate with a fancy dress ball.

The Mulcahys had an impressive mansion on Ailesbury Road, and the party was going to be a lavish affair. Sheila had told Mary and Nora that a small orchestra had already been engaged for the night, and that some guests were even going so far as to hire fancy dress costumes from a theatrical supplier in London's West End.

'Mexican sounds great!' enthused Mary as they sat at their shared desk. 'We could have those fancy fans, and flowers in our hair.'

'Isn't that more Spanish? And maybe *sombreros* are wrong

then? Is it only men who wear them?'

'What does it matter? If it's a fancy dress, you can wear anything.'

'Right. And you think Mexican is OK?' asked Nora. 'I mean, Panama is in Central America – I looked it up on the map.'

'Mexican, Spanish … sure isn't it all foreign?' answered Mary blithely. 'It'll be grand.'

They got out their English books for the next class and Nora considered her friend's reaction. *It'll be grand*. At times she wished that she could have Mary's easygoing approach to life. Nothing bothered her and she just enjoyed every pleasure that came her way. Nora worried that maybe she was too serious, that maybe even people like her cousin Alan might have some grounds for mocking her as a miniature suffragette.

But then again surely she shouldn't have to choose between having fun at a fancy dress party and still being able to care about people who weren't so lucky? And why shouldn't she enjoy life like any other girl her age but still believe that there was something badly wrong with a teacher like Miss Dillon being sacked?

All of the girls in Nora's class had been upset at the time, but she knew that Mary and Sheila and many of the other girls had moved on now. They had accepted the injustice without too much further thought, just as they accepted that it was normal for the government to imprison suffragettes – and just as they accepted that there would be a lock-out against workers who wanted to earn a living wage.

It was the kind of topic she could have discussed with Liam, but not with Mary or Sheila. And even though the girls were her friends she still hadn't felt able to tell them about Liam. *Why was that?* she wondered. But before she could reflect any further, their new teacher, Sister Regina, entered the classroom and the hubbub halted at once.

Sister Regina was much stricter than Miss Dillon had been, and Nora thought how much they had lost with the departure of their old teacher. *Well, other people could forget her, but I won't,* she resolved silently. *And I won't forget the promise I made either, that when the time is right I'll make a stand of which Miss Dillon would be proud.* Strengthened by the thought, she dismissed her earlier self doubts, sat forward in her desk and readied herself for whatever the day's class might bring.

Chapter 15

Liam watched Nora advance towards him, a smile on her face as she crossed the rehearsal room.

'We missed you on Tuesday night,' she said. 'Not like you to mitch!'

Liam had already explained to Brother Raymond about his father being imprisoned, and he had been surprisingly sympathetic, but Liam didn't want the other choir members to know his business, and so he replied casually:

'Couldn't help it.'

He could see that Nora was a little surprised by his response and he inclined his head towards the window alcove, indicating that she should join him there, where they could talk more privately.

'What's wrong?' she asked as soon as they were safely out of earshot of the others.

'It's Da. He's been arrested.'

'Oh, no!'

'The police lifted him on Monday. He's in Mountjoy Jail.'

'Oh my goodness. And what … what is he supposed to

have done?'

'He grappled with a DMP man at a picket line, so he was up for assault.'

'Oh Liam, that's … that's awful.'

'If it wasn't that it would have been something else. They were out to get him.'

'Really?'

'That's what he said.'

'And how long will he be in jail?'

Liam swallowed before he answered, not wanting to sound emotional. 'He got three months' hard labour.'

'Gosh.'

'Like I said, they were out to get him.'

'I'm so sorry, Liam, I really am.'

'Thanks,' he answered, touched by her obvious concern.

'So, what's your family going to do?'

Liam shrugged. 'What can we do? I'll have to help Ma as much as I can.'

'But, for … money … and food and everything?'

'Ma makes a few bob from her dressmaking. And I'll collect Da's strike pay – though that's not much.'

'Oh, Liam.'

He glanced away. He had told no one else in the choir, not wanting their sympathy, and now that he had told Nora she was really sad for him, which made him feel bad.

'We'll get food from the union as well as the strike pay. We won't starve,' he said, turning back to her and making his tone more upbeat.

Nora looked at him, and Liam could see that she wasn't convinced by his attempt to sound positive.

'It's not good though, is it?' she said.

Liam hesitated. Ever since the shock of the news on Monday he had been trying to keep up a brave face, but it was a relief to have someone with whom he could be honest.

'No, it's ... it's pretty bad.'

'And what happens to your father if the lockout ends while he's in prison? Will he get his job back when he's let out?'

'I don't know if they'd hold a job for someone who's in jail for fighting with a policeman.'

'They let Mr Larkin out early, maybe they'll let your dad out early too.'

'Ma has us praying for that.'

'I'll pray for it too, Liam. Every night, I promise.'

'Thanks. It's just ... like, my da is really tough and strong, but in prison ... you wouldn't know what they'd do to him.'

'I'm sure they won't mistreat him.'

'I hope you're right.'

'Liam, there's something I want to say, but ...'

'What?' he prompted when Nora hesitated.

'I don't want to offend you, but what you said earlier ...'

'About what?'

'About being short of money, and needing to get food. I'd

like to help.' Nora raised her hand to prevent Liam objecting. 'Please, just listen. We're really good friends, and friends are meant to help each other. I know it's not much, but I just got my pocket money for this week. Would you take it? Please? For your family.'

Liam felt a lump in his throat, and he blinked hard, trying to stop the tears that he felt welling up in his eyes.

'Please, Liam,' persisted Nora.

It was a really generous gesture, but something stopped him from taking cash from Nora, knowing that the pocket money had come from her father. Whatever about accepting a book as a gift, he couldn't take money. 'Thanks, Nora, you're … you're a great friend. But I can't.'

Nora looked at him, and Liam could see the uncertainty in her eyes.

'It's not that I'm not grateful, I really am. And you're brilliant to offer. But I can't take it.'

'Liam …'

'There's no need. We'll manage OK. Really, we will.'

He saw that Nora was about to reply, but Brother Raymond called the rehearsal to order, and Liam was relieved to be saved from further argument. He tapped Nora on the shoulder in thanks, then turned away, took out his sheet music and hoped he could leave his worries behind for the next two hours.

'What do you think, Mummy?' asked Nora as she entered the drawing room in her fancy dress outfit.

Her mother had helped her to acquire most of the items, but this was the first time that Nora had tried on the full costume and she was pleased to see her mother smiling approvingly.

'It's excellent, Nora,' she said. 'You'll be the belle of the ball!'

'Thanks, Mummy.'

Nora turned towards her father, who was engrossed in his newspaper.

'Thomas,' said her mother, and he lowered the paper distractedly, then smiled on seeing his daughter's costume.

'That's marvellous, Nora, really colourful.'

Nora thought that it actually *was* marvellous. She was wearing a long dress in red satin and black lace gloves. She had a full-size fan in one hand and castanets in the other, and the *sombrero* to top it all off. She knew that a *sombrero* wouldn't actually be worn with the rest of the costume, but she loved the big rounded hat, and as Mary said, it was fancy dress, so really you could wear anything you liked.

Her two brothers came into the room just then, and David sneered.

'That looks really stupid!'

'Yeah,' said David, slavishly echoing his older brother.

Nora decided to ignore them, feeling that little brothers talked rubbish most of the time, but she was pleased when her mother intervened.

'Mind your manners, Peter. You too, David.'

The boys looked a little taken aback, especially when her mother pointed towards the stairs. 'Up to your rooms and finish your homework, right now.'

Her brothers left sheepishly and, bringing things back to a happy footing, her father looked admiringly at her costume once again.

'I wouldn't be surprised if you won a prize for one of the best outfits,' he said.

'Do you think I might?' asked Nora.

'Absolutely – wouldn't be surprised at all. And when did you say this ball is?'

'Really, Thomas,' said Mummy in mild disapproval, but Nora didn't take exception to his being a little distracted.

'Tomorrow night,' she replied.

'Yes, of course. Sorry, Nora, my thoughts were elsewhere.'

'It's all right, Daddy.' And it was all right, for Nora knew that the lockout was causing all sorts of problems for the employers as well as the locked-out workers. She began to take off the sombrero and her gloves, and her father indicated the newspaper to her mother.

'Extraordinary scenes at the docks, according to *The Irish*

Times,' he said. 'It seems the clergy prevented the children being taken to England.'

'Proper order,' said her mother.

Liam had told Nora that there was a plan to send children of some of the locked-out workers to England temporarily, where they were to be fed and looked after by the families of English trade unionists. But some priests in Dublin had claimed that the children's faith would be in danger in England, and had led crowds of people to the docks, where they had blocked the children from boarding the ships.

'I'm not so sure,' said her father.

He rarely disagreed outright with his wife, but Nora could see that he was troubled by the article in the newspaper.

'It sounds to me like the priests showed a little too much vigour.'

'Their concern is for the children. Who knows what religion, if any, the families in England would have.'

'Mr Larkin says it's a poor religion that can't take a holiday,' said Nora.

Her mother turned to face her.

'Mr Larkin is hardly qualified in such matters, Nora.'

'Well … he is a Catholic himself, Mummy.'

'Then he shouldn't put the faith of children at risk,' said her mother sternly. She looked at Nora quizzically. 'And where did you learn to quote Mr Larkin?'

'I … eh … I heard a girl in school saying it,' answered Nora, hoping the explanation sounded convincing.

'Really?'

'Yes,' answered Nora, then, seeking to distract attention from herself, she turned to her father.

'Daddy, all this trouble with Mr Larkin and the lockout, is it going to end soon?'

'Difficult to say, Nora. If Mr Larkin continues getting support from England he may prolong the agony here for some time.'

Nora made sure to keep her voice reasonable. 'But, Daddy, could they not just let the men go back to work?'

'Not if they're members of a union.'

'Why not? Could they not let them *be* in a union and just pay them – I don't know … whatever is *fair*?'

'I wish we could, Nora. I hate the idea of anyone going hungry, but it's … it's complicated.'

'And not the kind of thing on which a young lady should exercise herself,' added her mother firmly.

Nora thought of Mrs Pankhurst, the leader of the suffragettes, who had been told that she shouldn't exercise herself in seeking votes for women. But she *had* exercised herself, despite being pursued by the police, and brought before the courts, and even sent to prison. Since first hearing of the suffragette movement from Miss Dillon, Nora had followed their exploits and found them inspiring, but she knew that this was not the time to say so.

'Now, I think you should take off your costume, dear,' said her mother, 'and hang it up for tomorrow night.'

Nora didn't want to get into a row, so she said 'Yes, Mummy,' politely. Then she left the room, still rooting for Mr Larkin, but with a little of the good somehow gone from the prospect of the fancy dress.

Chapter 16

Liam hungrily tucked into his plate of stew. It was over three weeks since his father had been jailed, and the lockout was in its ninth week, with money and food getting scarcer all the time. His mother did her best to stretch out the weekly food parcels from the union, and between that, the meagre strike pay, and whatever she could earn herself, the family managed somehow to survive.

Liam made a conscious effort not to wolf down the stew too obviously, so he slowed himself, relishing each precious mouthful. It had been Brother Raymond's idea to begin serving stew before rehearsals, and Liam was glad that he could count on a hot meal each Tuesday and Thursday night.

Brother Raymond claimed that the food was to warm the children up now that it was November and the weather had turned cold, but Liam suspected that this was just an excuse. The choirmaster had to be aware that many people in the city were going hungry because of the lockout, including some of his young pupils, and this way it was possible to distribute hot, nourishing food without it seeming like charity.

Liam chewed the meat, grateful to Brother Raymond for his thoughtfulness. He saw Nora come into the rehearsal room.

'Hello, Liam,' she said.

'Nora.'

Seeing Nora taking off her mittens, the choirmaster came over.

'Nora,' he said, 'care for a warming plate of stew?'

Liam noted a tiny hesitation before Nora smiled and nodded.

'Yes, thank you, Brother, that would be lovely.'

She probably had a full dinner before she came here, but she knows what's going on, Liam thought. This was only the second night that the food had been served, and Liam had noticed some of the more middle-class children being a bit sniffy and declining to eat the stew.

Nora took her plate and began to eat with apparent relish, and Liam felt a surge of admiration for her. As one of the wealthiest children in the choir she was sending out a message that there was nothing wrong with eating the food provided. He saw Brother Raymond smiling approvingly, and he guessed that the choirmaster also knew what Nora was doing.

Liam finished his stew, then looked up as Brother Raymond cleared his throat and addressed the choir.

'Your attention, boys and girls. No, it's all right, those of you eating may continue, but I do have an important announcement.' He paused dramatically, and Liam smiled to himself, knowing how the choirmaster enjoyed his theatrical flourishes.

'We have been chosen,' said Brother Raymond, 'chosen, I might add, from *many* available choirs, to perform at a charity concert at the Mansion House in three weeks time. It's a considerable honour, and we need to rehearse assiduously – most assiduously.'

Brother Raymond loved using big words, like 'assiduously'. But he wasn't wrong about the honour, though, because the Mansion House was the home of the Lord Mayor of Dublin, and to perform there *was* a big thing.

'So, a date to remember, boys and girls: Saturday, November the twenty-ninth. And I expect no one to miss a single rehearsal between now and then. Not a single one. Understood?'

'Yes, Brother!' chanted Liam, along with everybody else.

'Very well, rehearsals begin in five minutes.'

'That's great, isn't it?' said Nora.

'Brilliant,' answered Liam. It was good to have something to look forward to, and a big concert like this would help to distract him from his other worries.

'Lovely stew,' said Nora, pushing away her empty plate.

'Yeah, it was really good,' said Liam, noting that a couple of the wealthier children had followed Nora's example and taken the stew. 'So, how are things going for your Panama Canal party?' he asked.

'Really well,' answered Nora, but before she could elaborate, Maurice Fitzgerald entered the room excitedly.

He normally arrived at least five minutes before rehearsals began, but tonight he had obviously been side-tracked, and Liam could see at once that he had some sort of news to tell.

'Have you heard?' the boy asked breathlessly.

'Heard what?'

'About Mr Larkin?'

'What about him?' asked Liam worriedly. He knew that Larkin was up in court yet again, and a lot was riding on what happened there.

'His trial has finished.'

Liam looked at the other boy anxiously 'Was he found guilty or not guilty?'

'Guilty!'

Liam felt his heart sink, but he asked the question that he knew had to be asked. 'What was the sentence?'

'Seven months in prison!' answered Maurice, clearly delighted to be the bearer of such dramatic news. Liam looked away, unable to bear the other boy's excitement. This could be a disaster. After all the pain and sacrifice, now they had lost their leader. And with their leader gone, how were they going to survive the lockout and beat the employers?

Chapter 17

Nora licked the mixture of fresh cream and icing sugar from her fingers as she finished her second cream slice. It was usual when performing at weddings for the singers to be provided with food and drink, and the choir had tucked into beef and Yorkshire pudding, wedding cake, and now the unexpected treat of cream slices in a small side-room off the main hotel ballroom where the wedding meal was being served. They had already sung at the church, and would be performing again after the speeches, but for now they could relax.

'Do you think we might hear some tango music at this?' asked Liam.

'Have you seen the musicians?'

'No.'

Nora grimaced. 'I saw them outside. I'd say it'll be old time waltzes.'

Nora and Liam loved the musical rhythms of the Latin American dance that was rapidly growing in popularity. A group of Argentine musicians had been brought in specially for the Panama Party a few weeks previously and their music had been the highlight of the evening. The party itself had been lavish and colourful and, despite not winning any prizes for her fancy dress, Nora had enjoyed herself thoroughly and had told Liam all about it at the next rehearsal.

Now, he looked disappointed that they weren't likely to hear any tango at the reception. 'You'd get sick of old-time waltzes, wouldn't you?' he said.

'You would a bit.'

'Still, the grub was great. And a bob each for singing is pretty good.'

'Very good,' agreed Nora.

They had each been given a shilling by the best man after the church ceremony, and once they had sung again after the speeches they would be free to go, making it a well-paid day's work. Nora was sure that it was money badly needed by Liam for his family, but, although it was extra pocket money for her, she didn't dare offer to give it to him, after his last refusal.

'Another one, Nora?' Liam held out the cake plate.

Nora shook her head. As much as she loved cream slices, she just couldn't manage a third. A thought struck her. The cream slices would surely be a treat for Liam's sisters. On the other hand, she didn't want him to feel humiliated, which he might be if she suggested taking left-over food.

She looked at the three-tiered cake stands that were still half full of wedding cake and cream slices. 'I'm going to bring these home for my brothers,' she said, reaching out and wrapping two slices of cake in a napkin. 'Why don't you take some for your sisters?'

She could see at once that Liam was taken by the idea, but he also looked a little uncertain.

'Do you think that's OK? They wouldn't think we were stealing?' he asked.

'Why would they think that? They were put there for us to eat, weren't they?'

'Yeah, you're right,' said Liam, and he wrapped up a good few slices of cake. If he thought it strange that Nora was bringing home cake for two brothers that she normally gave out about, he said nothing.

Nora was pleased that her idea had worked. She had learned recently that there was a fine line between helping a friend in need and appearing to be doling out charity. She really admired Brother Raymond for how he had come up with the scheme of serving the stew. He had increased the number of rehearsals too, now that the big concert in the Mansion House was only a week away, but Nora suspected that in part the extra rehearsals were to ensure that choir members like Liam were guaranteed hot meals that they wouldn't have at home.

Liam finished loading his pockets with cake, then he turned to Nora and smiled. 'My sisters will be delighted.'

Nora tried to smile back, but suddenly the effort of

pretending was too much.

'Are things really bad, Liam?' she asked.

Liam's smile vanished. He looked at her, then nodded his head slowly.

'Pretty bad. Larkin is back in England trying to get support. If he doesn't get it I don't know what will happen.'

Nora had heard from her father that with public opinion strongly sympathetic to the plight of the locked out workers – and with voters heeding a call to vote against the ruling Liberal Party in by-elections – the government had given in to pressure and released Mr Larkin seventeen days into his latest sentence. But Liam's father and many other workers were still in prison.

'And … and your family, Liam?'

Again he hesitated. Nora knew that she mustn't push him. But he was her friend and she wanted him to know that he could talk to her if he wanted to. She waited, allowing Liam to decide how to respond. He breathed out and looked at her.

'It's not good, Nora. The work Ma used to get has dried up. If Da was out of jail he'd look out for us somehow, but he can't do anything from inside Mountjoy.'

'So how do you manage?'

'Ma had to use the burial money,' said Liam.

'What's that?'

'You know, money for when you die and have to pay to be buried?'

Liam seemed surprised that Nora had never heard of it.

'Even people much poorer than us try to put away something, maybe only a penny a week, as burial money. That way, if someone in the family dies they won't have to go in a pauper's grave.'

Nora tried to imagine what it would feel like if her father, or anyone in her family, had to be buried by charity, in an unmarked grave with no headstone or flowers. It was a horrible thought, and she knew that the situation must be really bad if the family of a tradesman like Liam's father was so desperate that they had to use their burial money for food.

'Have you no relations who could help out till your dad is released?' she asked.

'All my aunts and uncles in Dublin are locked out too. They have to try and feed their own families and my granny as well.'

'Right.'

'My ma's sister, Aunt Molly, lives down the country. She's going to try and send us up some food.'

'Where does she live?'

'Hazelwood Farm. It's near Ballinacargy, in County Westmeath.'

'That's miles away. How will she get food to Dublin?'

'A friend of Da's is a carter. He's locked out of work, but he's going to get a horse and cart and drive down.'

'How far is it?'

'Sixty or seventy miles, I think. It'll take him a few days.'

Nora looked at Liam and she felt a swell of mixed emotions. Part of her felt really sorry for him, and the awful situation his family faced. And part of her really admired him, and the way he just got on with things without moaning. This was the first time that he had revealed his home situation in this kind of detail however, and Nora felt flattered that he had confided in her.

'It's all so unfair, Liam, I wish I could help,' she said.

'Thanks. But sure there's nothing you can do.'

'Maybe there is,' said Nora, then, before she lost her nerve, she took from her pocket the shilling that the best man had paid her and placed it on the table. 'Take this, please. I don't need it and it will help till the food arrives from Westmeath.'

Liam looked at her without speaking, and Nora pushed the coin closer to him.

'Please, Liam, don't be annoyed. Friends help each other out. You'd help me if I needed it – that's how we met in the first place, remember?'

'That was different.'

'It wasn't, really. I was in trouble and you helped me. Now you're in trouble – let me help you.'

Liam hesitated, and Nora decided to press her case.

'Make it a loan if you don't want to take money. A loan till your dad is out of jail and back working. OK?'

To Nora's surprise she saw Liam's eyes moistening, then he looked away.

'I won't forget this, Nora,' he said after a moment. 'I'll never forget this.' Then he picked up the coin and put it in his pocket, and to her further surprise, Nora felt the tears welling up in her own eyes.

Chapter 18

'Go to your choir practice, Liam. Go on, I'm all right.'

'But what are we going to do, Ma?'

'We'll manage somehow,' answered his mother, although Liam could see that she was struggling to sound convincing. 'It will be all right, pet, really.'

But as Liam looked away from his mother, who was wrapped up in her overcoat to save lighting the fire, he knew that things wouldn't be all right. Sean, the carter friend of Da's who had volunteered to get the supplies from Ballinacargy, had been involved in a clash between locked-out workers and scabs, and had had his arm broken by a blow from a police baton.

They had been counting on the food that Aunt Molly had organised. Liam had seen how his mother denied herself food so that there would be more for him and his sisters. He looked back at her now, her normally happy face pale and drawn in the flickering glow from the single gas lamp that lit the front room.

'There must be something we can do, Ma. Is there no other carter who could go down for us?'

'It's a very long journey, Liam. It's not easy to get someone to go all that way, though Sean said that he'd ask around.'

'We can't just hope for the best, Ma.'

'We'll pray to Our Lady. She's never let us down yet.'

Liam was about to protest further, but Ma raised her hand 'Go on with you now. I won't have you late for your rehearsal. Go on.'

Liam knew better than to argue further, and he kissed his mother goodbye, then set off for rehearsals. The weather had turned bitterly cold, but he barely noticed as he moved briskly along the cobbled streets, his mind racing. By the time he turned into Sackville Place and approached the rehearsal room he had decided on a course of action.

He paused at the foot of the stairs, getting his nerve up for what he had to do next. He dreaded confronting Brother Raymond, but he knew what was required and, steeling himself, he climbed the stairs and walked into the rehearsal room. It was pleasantly warm after the icy air outside and there was an enticing smell from the stew that was being served. Normally Liam's mouth would have been watering, but right now he was too nervous to think about food, and before he could falter, he crossed to Brother Raymond.

'Excuse me, Brother.'

'Liam.'

'Could I … could I talk to you for a minute?'

'Of course.' The choir master turned to the nearby Maurice Fitzsimons and indicated the soup bowls. 'Maurice, would you look after distributing the stew?'

'Yes, Brother,' Maurice answered, taking the ladle from him.

Brother Raymond put his hand on Liam's shoulder and gently ushered him to the far end of the room where they couldn't be heard, although Liam was aware that the other choir members were all watching them.

'So, Liam, what's wrong?'

Liam hesitated.

'What is it?'

'I'm really, really sorry, Brother, but I'm not going to be able to sing at the Mansion House on Saturday.'

'Oh?'

'I know it's only two days away, and we've put in loads of work, and I'm really sorry, Brother, but I've only just found out.'

'Found out what?'

Liam had already decided that he couldn't tell anyone what he had planned, but he hated lying to the Brother. 'I, eh … it's my family, Brother. There's something … something we have to do next Saturday. I'm sorry, Brother, but we've just no choice.'

Liam bit his lip, nervously waiting for the backlash.

Brother Raymond tended to get very angry if anyone pulled out of important performances at short notice, and he looked searchingly at Liam now. Liam was about to try and expand on his explanations when, to his surprise, Brother Raymond spoke gently.

'Is it anything I can help with, Liam?'

'Eh, no … no, not really, Brother.'

'Are you sure?'

Liam couldn't believe that he wasn't in trouble, and in his relief he found himself blabbing. 'Yes, I'm sure but … but thanks very much all the same, Brother, thank you.'

'I won't press you, Liam. I know you wouldn't miss singing for the Lord Mayor if you could possibly avoid it.'

'No, Brother, definitely not.'

'But if there's something I can help your family with, don't be afraid to ask. All right?'

'Yes, Brother. Thanks.'

Brother Raymond nodded, then he patted Liam on the shoulder. 'Make sure to have some stew before we start. It'll warm you up.'

'I will, Brother,' answered Liam, then he breathed out, relieved and still a little in shock at the response.

✳   ✳   ✳

Nora watched curiously as Brother Raymond left Liam and returned to supervising the distribution of the stew. She knew from their conversation that something must be up, and she quickly crossed the room to be at Liam's side.

'Are you OK?' she asked.

'Yeah.'

'Are you sure?'

'I'm kind of surprised. I thought Raymond was going to take my head off.'

'Why?'

'Because I can't sing in the Mansion House on Saturday.'

Nora was shocked. This was a big occasion for the choir, and Liam had been so excited at singing for the Lord Mayor.

'Why not?' she asked.

'That carter friend of my da's was injured. He can't go to Ballinacargy.'

'Oh no.'

'We really need that stuff, Nora. I'm going to go instead.'

'Your mother will never let you.'

'I won't tell her.'

'But … but you can't drive a cart to Westmeath, can you?'

'No. But I can jump a train. I have to do something, Nora, my little sister was crying last night because she was hungry.'

Nora was horrified at the idea of Peg crying, yet she couldn't help but think of the practicalities.

'But … how would you get the food back to Dublin?'

'I'll jump another train.'

Nora's head was reeling. Other than in story books, she had

never heard of anyone jumping a train.

'But how will you carry it?'

'In my pockets, in my arms. Even if I can't take it all, I'll take as much as I can.'

Nora thought of Liam's little sister crying with hunger, and she knew that she had to act. She took a deep breath, then looked at Liam.

'I'll come with you,' she said. 'I'll help you carry it back.'

Liam stared at her, and she could see that he was amazed.

'You ... you can't, Nora. You have the concert.'

'I'll skip it. I'll ... I'll cover somehow with Mummy; we'll go to Westmeath together.'

'No! You can't, Nora.'

Nora was taken aback by the strength of Liam's reaction.

'Please. You're a great friend, Nora, you're really dead sound. But I can't drag you into this.'

'You're not dragging me, I want to help.'

'I know, and I'm really grateful. But this is something I have to do. You can't miss the concert.'

'There'll be other concerts.'

Liam looked at her, his face determined. 'No. I'm not getting you into huge trouble with your parents, and that's what would happen.'

Nora was about to argue, but Liam raised his hand to stop her.

'Thanks all the same. But I'm going on my own.'

He said it with an air of finality, then gestured towards where the food was being served. 'I'm hungry. I'm going to get some stew.'

Nora watched him walking away. She felt confused by her own emotions. Partly she was shocked at the offer she had made, partly disappointed that Liam had refused her help. And, if she were honest, part of her was relieved – the idea of defying her parents and taking off to Westmeath *was* pretty frightening. But mostly she felt dissatisfied. People were starving, battles were being fought, and she was watching – safely and comfortably – and as usual from the sidelines.

She stood there, unmoving, aware of Liam tucking hungrily into the stew, and she realised that the time for watching was over. She wasn't sure what she was going to do, but this time she simply had to do something.

PART THREE

ENDGAME

Chapter 19

Liam stared out the window of the speeding train, hoping not to be noticed. The carriage was still only about half full, and earlier he had discreetly taken a window seat, facing forward. The morning sunshine was not strong enough yet to melt the heavy frost from the night before, and the countryside through which the train travelled westwards had a frozen, icy beauty about it. But despite admiring the ever-changing winter scene unfolding before his view, Liam couldn't relax. Any minute now a conductor must surely enter the carriage to check tickets, and that would be a tricky moment.

So far, everything had gone to plan. He had set off for school at his usual time, but as soon as he was out of sight of his house, had turned towards the station. With Broadstone depot practically on his doorstep, Liam was very familiar with its many tracks and marshalling yards. He had hidden his school-bag under a stack of ballast stones, then mounted the platform for the Sligo-bound train, coming from the direction of the goods yards and thus avoiding the ticket collector at the main concourse of the station.

Before leaving home he had given Eileen, his eldest sister, a note for his ma. He had made Eileen promise not to hand it over until after she came home from school this afternoon. By then Liam hoped to have ridden the train to Mullingar and made his way the final eleven miles from there to Ballinacargy. In the letter he told his mother not to worry, and that he would get back to Dublin with the precious supplies as quickly as possible. Eileen tried to quiz him about what was going on, but he had insisted that she had to trust him, and that he was doing something that would mean food for the family.

Now, as the train clattered along the tracks, Liam tried not to show any nervousness. He sat in his window seat, the carriage warm and cosy in contrast to the frozen fields that whistled by outside the glass. He caught a movement from the corner of his eye, and glancing around, felt a sudden thumping in his chest. The ticket collector had entered their carriage. Liam had deliberately chosen the middle of the carriage so that he wouldn't be among the first to be asked for tickets. He rose, as casually as he could. He stepped into the passageway between the seats, making sure not to catch the eye of the heavy-set ticket collector, and made for the toilets.

Liam had picked a carriage that was near to the toilets, hoping to hide in there until the ticket collector had moved on to the next carriage. He walked along the passageway now, forcing himself not to rush. He felt as though the ticket collector's eyes were burning into his back, but he knew that was probably just his imagination and he resisted the temptation to glance behind him.

He prayed that there wouldn't be someone already in the toilet as he made for the sliding door at the end of the carriage. He pulled it across, closed it after himself, then anxiously tried the handle of the adjacent toilet.

The handle swung down, and Liam felt a surge of relief. He stepped into the toilet and locked the door. It was colder here and bumpier too, and Liam had to brace himself to prevent being banged against the walls. *How long should I stay here to be sure the ticket collector has moved on? Better to stay a good while rather than risk running into him,* he thought. *Then again, if I stay too long I might draw attention if other passengers want to use the toilet.*

He didn't know how long he stood there, his mouth dry and his pulses racing. Suddenly he was startled by a loud knocking on the door.

'Ticket, please!'

Liam felt his heart pounding wildly but he tried not to panic.

'I'll … I'll be out in a while.'

'How long are you going to be?'

'A few more minutes,' answered Liam, trying to keep his voice normal as he played for time.

'I can't be waiting that long,' said the collector. 'Slide your ticket under the door.'

Liam's mind raced as he tried to find an answer. 'Can I … can I bring it up the carriage to you when I'm finished here?' he suggested.

'No. Open the door and show me your ticket, or slide it under the door. But I want to see a ticket – now!'

Nora's mind was miles away, but she managed to give the impression of paying attention as she chanted out her poetry with the other girls in English class. They were reciting Thomas Grey's *Elegy in a Country Churchyard*, a poem she really liked and, knowing the verses by heart, Nora was able to call them out with the other girls while her mind was elsewhere.

She had been upset the night before by the idea of Liam's little sister crying because she was hungry. Upset, but frustrated too that Liam had declined her offer to go with him to Ballinacargy. Liam was only trying to protect her, of course, but she was tired of being protected.

Just now, her teacher, Sister Regina, had tried to protect her from the imagined evils of the suffragette movement. Not surprisingly, Sister Regina was far more conservative than Miss Dillon had been, and the middle-aged nun had just read out to the class some extracts from Sir Almroth Wright's new book, *The Unexpurgated Case Against Woman Suffrage*. Nora had tried to argue against the author's views, but Sister Regina had told her to sit down, and had sharply pointed out that when she wanted to conduct a debate, she would inform Nora.

Nora was inwardly seething, but seething wasn't going to get her anywhere. Action was the only way to change things. And there *was* a course of action that would make up for a lot of frustration. *But had she the nerve to do it?* Because, despite Liam's views, or Sister Regina's views, she *could* act here. She could pretend to go to the concert in the Mansion House tomorrow morning – but instead follow Liam to Ballinacargy and help him bring the food home. If she did it, it would be the most rebellious thing she had ever done in her life, and there would be hell to pay afterwards. Just then she looked up and saw the nun's thin-lipped, self-satisfied face as she led the girls in the poem. And suddenly, without doubt, Nora knew that she had to rebel.

✳ ✳ ✳

Liam opened the toilet door to find the ticket collector standing directly before him. 'Where's your ticket?' the man challenged him.

'I can't find it,' answered Liam. 'I put it into my trousers pocket, but it must have fallen out.'

'Is that the best you can do?' asked the ticket collector, his tone sarcastic.

Liam concentrated on trying to sound innocent. 'Maybe you've heard that before, but really, I had the ticket when I got on.'

The man looked at him for a moment without speaking, and Liam hoped that perhaps he was winning him around.

'Fair enough,' said the ticket collector. 'If you bought a ticket, you bought a ticket.'

'Thanks, mister,' said Liam gratefully.

'One last question?'

'Yes?'

'What did the ticket cost?'

Liam felt his stomach tighten. He had never bought a railway ticket; Da always did that when the family was travelling. *What might it cost to travel from Dublin to Mullingar? Sixpence? Nine pence? A shilling?*

'Well?'

'Nine pence,' answered Liam.

'Lying pup!' said the man, then he grabbed Liam roughly by the shoulder. 'You're off the train when we stop in Enfield. The police can deal with you.'

'I have to get to my aunt's,' pleaded Liam, 'it's really important.'

'Save the hard luck story. I've heard them all.'

'I'm collecting food,' persisted Liam, 'my sisters are hungry.'

'Then you should have bought a ticket like everyone else.'

Liam was about to argue further but the man raised a podgy finger and pointed it threateningly in his face. 'Shut your mouth, you little liar, or I'll shut it for you!'

Liam said nothing, then the man pushed him forward.

'Down that way, you can wait in the guard's van.'

Liam stepped through the sliding door into the next carriage, followed by the ticket collector. He didn't want the disgrace of looking like the man's prisoner, so he kept several paces ahead of him as they made their way through the carriage. They passed through another set of sliding doors and into a third carriage and Liam felt the train beginning to slow down.

'Must be approaching Enfield,' he heard one passenger saying to another. Liam continued on down the carriage, then pulled back the next sliding door. He held it open for the ticket collector. Just before the man stepped through, Liam looked in horror back up the carriage.

'Oh my God!' he cried.

The ticket collector looked around to see what had caused Liam's distress. While the man was distracted, Liam quickly put his foot behind the conductor's leg, then suddenly pushed with all his strength against the man. Completely taken by surprise, the ticket collector fell backwards, tripping over Liam's foot and losing his balance.

Liam saw him falling heavily to the floor, and he swiftly pulled the sliding door shut and ran across the small vestibule to undo the catch for the outside door of the train. He pulled hard, but the catch was stiff and didn't yield. Driven on by fear of the ticket collector, Liam pulled again at the catch. He used every ounce of his strength, and this time the catch came down and the door suddenly swung open. Liam was blown back by a freezing gust of smoke-filled wind.

To his horror, he saw that while the train was definitely slowing down, it was still going far more quickly than he would have liked. Trying to control his fear, Liam looked out the open door of the carriage. There was an embankment alongside the track. It might have been soft and grassy in the summer, but right now it looked hard and frosty in the morning sunlight and not likely to cushion his fall very much if he jumped. Then he heard the sound of the sliding door being pulled back and he knew that it had to be the ticket collector.

Still, the thought of jumping terrified him. He stood at the doorway, willing himself to leap. From the corner of his eye he saw the ticket collector moving towards him, his face red and angry. He had only a split second to weigh up his choices. *Jump and risk being injured. Don't jump and face the ticket collector.*

And if the man handed Liam over to the police, there was no way of bringing home the food.

He jumped. He felt a sudden roaring of wind in his ears, then he hit the embankment and lost his balance. The force of his landing jolted him badly, but he tried to roll forward in the same direction that the train was travelling, hoping that this would help to break his fall. He found himself sliding down the frosty embankment, then he came to a stop. His shoulder was throbbing, his neck felt sprained, and his hip was sore from where it had scraped along the ground.

Ignoring his aches for the moment, he quickly looked up to see what was happening with the train. The good news was that the ticket collector hadn't jumped off after him and the train was continuing on its way. But it was slowing down considerably, and Liam realised that it mustn't be too far to Enfield station. And when it stopped there the ticket collector might well report him to the police. *Time to get out of here.* He picked himself up gingerly and felt his shoulder and his hip. He didn't appear to have broken anything. His clothes were wet from sliding along the frosty ground, but they hadn't been ripped, and Liam brushed off the ice and leaves that had attached to him, then looked around to get his bearings.

The embankment gave way to a large field, and in a corner of the field, about a hundred yards away, there was a gate, behind which Liam could see a laneway. Liam turned away from the embankment, crossed a narrow ditch into the field and began to run towards the gate.

❋　❋　❋

'Are you mad, Nora?' asked Mary incredulously. 'Your mum will kill you!'

Nora couldn't help but smile at the expression on her friend's face as they made their way from one classroom to another.

'She won't if she doesn't find out.'

'How could she not find out?'

'If I head for Ballinacargy first thing in the morning I could get back by tomorrow night.'

'But you might never find this farm. Or suppose you can't get a train back in time.'

'Well, if that happens, that's where you come in.'

'What?' Mary stopped in the corridor and looked quizzically at Nora.

Nora paused, knowing that how she handled this could be really important. She had already apologised to Mary for not telling her about Liam until now, and to Mary's credit she had scolded Nora briefly, but then grudgingly accepted Nora's explanation about why she had kept quiet about her friendship with a working class boy.

'I need you to be a friend to me tomorrow, Mary.'

'What does that mean?'

'If I don't get back in time, I want you to give a letter to my parents. I don't want them worried sick. It will just explain where I'm gone in case I get held up.'

'I'll be killed for getting involved,' said Mary.

'You won't.' Nora laid her hand reassuringly on her friend's arm. 'If I get back in time, I'll telephone you, and you can tear up the letter. If I don't, you just push the letter under our door and no one will know who I got to deliver it.'

'They'll know it was one of your friends.'

'They won't know which one. And I'm never going to tell.'

Mary looked dubious. 'I don't know …'

'There are girls like us going hungry, Mary. Liam's little sister, Peg, is only three. She was crying at night because they haven't enough food.'

'God!'

'Remember what Miss Dillon told us? That we can change the world? But that they'll try to stop us, just because we're girls? Well this is our chance to prove them wrong. To *do* something for once.'

Nora could see that Mary was swayed, but still her friend said nothing.

'I'm doing this for Liam and his family,' said Nora. 'But I'm doing it for Miss Dillon too. I hate what the school did to her. And if Miss Dillon was a girl like us she'd take action. Well I'm going to now, in her honour. So, will you do it?'

Mary looked at her, then nodded. 'Yes,' she said softly. Then she nodded more vigorously. 'Yes, I will!'

Liam walked quickly, trying to keep himself warm. The sun that had made the frost sparkle had now been replaced by heavy clouds, and the first traces of snow were starting to fall in feathery wisps. Normally Liam loved snowy weather – it meant snowball fights and the chance of school being closed due to burst pipes – but as he strode along the canal towpath heading west, a snow-covered route was the last thing he needed.

Liam didn't know how far he was from Mullingar, and after he had earlier made his way across the field beside the embankment, he had had to fight back a feeling of despair at being stranded. But despairing would get him nowhere, and he had told himself that the family was relying on him, and that he had to pull himself together. Somehow he had to get to Ballinacargy, and he decided that his best bet was to continue west along the canal towpath.

He carefully skirted the small town of Enfield, giving the train station a wide berth, then found his way back to the Royal Canal, which he knew went all the way to the River Shannon. He had once heard his da saying that the railway had been built on land that originally belonged to the canal company, which was why the rail line and the canal had run side by side since the train had left Dublin.

By following the towpath, he reasoned that sooner or later he had to reach a town with a train station, and he would try to jump a train there that would take him on to Mullingar.

It wasn't a great plan. The next town could be many miles away. The train mightn't stop there. And even if it did, it mightn't be easy to board unseen at a country station. But there was no point worrying about any of those things right now. Whatever it took, he simply had to reach Aunt Molly's farm. He put thoughts of failure from his mind and walked faster along the towpath as the temperature dipped and the snow got steadily heavier.

Nora glanced around anxiously to make sure that no one in the school locker room was watching, then she emptied her hockey clothes out of her sports bag and pushed the hockey gear to the back of her locker. She folded up the canvas sports bag as tightly as she could, then slipped it into her schoolbag. Tomorrow she would bring it with her when she made for Ballinacargy, where she could fill it with some of the food that Liam needed to bring back to Dublin.

She walked out of the locker room without anybody having seen her taking the sports bag, and she headed back towards her classroom, nervous at what she was taking on, but excited too, and satisfied that at last she was acting instead of talking.

The rest of her plans were all in place. She had already written the letter that she hoped would never have to be delivered to her parents, and given it to Mary. When she got home this afternoon she would empty her piggy bank so that she would have enough money for the train tomorrow. She would eat a big breakfast in the morning to give her energy, wear warm clothes, and bring a pair of strong, comfortable shoes in case she had to do a lot of walking.

Was there anything she was overlooking? If there was, she couldn't think of what it might be. Besides, with a journey into the unknown you couldn't plan everything in advance, you had to let a certain amount just happen. Satisfied that she had prepared as much as she could, she dismissed her worries, dropped off the schoolbag at her classroom, then made for the canteen with a spring in her step.

Liam marched through the snow, which was deeper now and covering the countryside in a blanket of white. It crunched underfoot as he walked along the towpath, but otherwise all was quiet, as though the falling snow was not only covering the landscape but silencing it as well.

Despite moving at a brisk pace, Liam's hands, face and legs felt cold from their exposure to the icy air. He found himself wishing that he was a year or two older, when he would have made the move from short to long trousers. As the snow settled in his hair he wished too that he had worn his school cap, but he had hidden the cap in his schoolbag back at Broadstone station, not wanting to draw attention to the fact that he was a schoolboy who should have been at classes today.

He strode along the towpath, impressed, despite all his problems, with the vista unfolding before him. This was a particularly broad and stately stretch of canal, with tall trees bounding the waterway on both sides, their branches covered in snow and stretching towards the sky like spindly white arms.

He tried to figure out how much ground he had covered. It must have been over an hour now since he had jumped from the train. Allowing for skirting the town of Enfield, and then walking quickly, he reckoned that he should have travelled between three and four miles.

Surely another hour's walk would bring him to some kind of town, he thought, although of course there could be no guarantee of that.

Just then he saw what looked like the outline of a building up ahead on his left and he picked up his pace even further. Drawing near, his hopes began to rise as he saw a couple of railway sidings and he realised that he was approaching a station. He slowed down, not wanting to draw attention to himself, and he proceeded more carefully, studying the station and the impressive house that rose behind it, from his vantage point across the width of the canal.

A sign proclaimed the place to be Moyvalley, but the station itself was small and there were no passengers on the platform. Liam could see smoke rising from the roof of the station house, however, and he reasoned that any passengers would be installed in the warmth of the waiting room.

Liam came to a halt and considered his options. This wasn't the kind of station he wanted. He needed somewhere that would be bustling – a large country town that would have passengers milling about the platform – in order to provide the cover he needed to sneak onto the train.

He stood there a moment, disappointment welling up inside him, but he forced himself not to give in to it. He would have liked to heat himself up at the waiting room fire, but he couldn't risk attracting the stationmaster's attention. Instead he turned away and followed the towpath, which led under an arched bridge. It was a fine, solid structure, and sheltering under it briefly, Liam realised that a main road probably ran overhead. Should he try his luck seeking a lift on the road? Or was it better to stay with the canal, knowing that it led west, in the direction he required?

He considered the choices, then found himself getting colder as he stood still, and he quickly made up his mind. He would take his chances with the canal. He moved on and rounded a bend. To his surprise he saw a country inn with an adjacent quay up ahead. A full length barge lay alongside the quay, its chimney belching forth a plume of black smoke. There was a group of bargemen offloading kegs of beer for the inn, and several of them looked at him inquisitively as he approached.

'Good morning,' said Liam, trying to sound as if walking along in the snow was nothing out of the ordinary.

'Morning,' answered the first of the bargemen.

'You're a hardy lad,' said another man, who had a strong

Dublin accent.

'Do you know what the next station is?' asked Liam.

'Hill of Down,' answered the first man.

Liam had never heard of it. 'And after that?'

'After that, Killucan.'

Liam had never heard of that either, which meant that neither of them was likely to be busy.

'Do you know how far we are from Mullingar?' he asked

'Twenty-one miles,' said the second man, looking enquiringly at Liam. 'That's a Dublin accent,' he said. 'What are you doing out here?'

'I, eh … I lost my train fare, so I'm walking,' Liam improvised.

One of the other men came forward and looked searchingly at Liam. 'Aren't you Billy O'Meara's young fella?' he asked.

Liam hesitated as he tried to figure out how best to respond.

'You're the spit of your aul' fella,' said the bargeman, and suddenly Liam's intention to make up a story dissolved. He was alone, he was cold, he was stranded over thirty miles from Ballinacargy – and here was someone who knew his father and who might help him.

'Yes,' he answered, 'I'm his son, Liam.'

'So what are you doing around here, Liam?'

Now that he had decided to tell the truth, Liam felt a sense of relief, and in a sudden torrent of words he spilled out the whole story. At the end of it, the man who had recognised Liam held out his hand for Liam to shake.

'I'm Tim Morrissey,' he said. 'I used to play hurling with your da.'

'Yeah?'

'I still have the marks to prove it! Hold on, Liam, till I have a word with the skipper.' He turned to one of the other bargemen. 'Jack, give Liam here a mug of brew while he's waiting.'

The first man moved off to talk to an older man at the far end of the barge, while the man addressed as Jack briefly went into the galley, then returned to Liam with a steaming mug of tea and a plate of gur cake, which he placed on the side of the barge.

'Get that into you, son,' he said, 'you look like you could do with warming up.'

'Thanks, mister,' said Liam, cupping his hands gratefully around the mug before swallowing the hot strong tea and biting into the sweet-tasting cake.

Tim returned and placed his hand on Liam's shoulder. 'OK, Liam, here's the story. We're not going as far as Ballinacargy. But if you want, you can have a lift with us to Mullingar.'

'Thanks, that would be great.'

'We're mooring there overnight. You can kip on the barge and make for Ballinacargy in the morning, if the roads aren't snowed under.'

'Thanks a million, that's really great.'

'Your aul' lad is sound as a pound. Sure we couldn't see you stuck. OK, hop up on the barge, we've finished our delivery here.'

'Brilliant,' cried Liam. He took another quick slug of the tea and a mouthful of gur cake, then climbed up onto the boat.

The bargemen untied the ropes and cast off from the quay. The engine revved up, plumes of thick black smoke erupting from the chimney, and Liam felt a surge of exhilaration as they pulled out into midstream, then headed off in the direction of Mullingar.

✳   ✳   ✳

Nora peered worriedly out of her bedroom window at the lightly falling snow. It was ten o'clock at night now and the snowfall was finally easing off, but Dublin was still covered in a carpet of white. Nora hoped it hadn't affected Liam's attempt to get to Westmeath, and that it wouldn't prevent her from travelling after him in the morning.

Her plans were all in place now but snow was the one thing on which she hadn't counted. All she could do was hope for the best. No, she thought, she could do better than that, she could pray.

She went down on her knees, the carpet soft and deep beneath her, and she said her night prayers. Then she added prayers for Mr O'Meara, Liam's father, as she had every night since he had been jailed. She prayed for Liam too, that he was safe and well and had made it to his aunt's. And finally she prayed for herself, that she would be brave tomorrow and that she wouldn't fail her friend.

She paused, added 'Please, God, don't let me down,' then she rose, turned off the gas lamp and jumped into bed, eager to get a good night's rest before tomorrow's adventures.

✳   ✳   ✳

Liam lay on a makeshift bed of blankets and cushions in the forward section of the barge. He felt warm and cosy as he listened to the sound of water lapping between the side of the barge and the icy wall of the quayside at the canal harbour in Mullingar. There was a faint glow of lamplight coming through the frame of the door leading back to the main cabin, where Tim and the other bargemen were drinking whiskey, their occasional laughter carrying to Liam's ears as he stretched out, contented and drowsy.

The barge had reached Mullingar just as the light had failed, and Liam had really enjoyed the adventure of travelling by boat. He had even been allowed to help with the lock gates when they navigated the extended set of locks through which the canal ascended near Killucan. It had been fun to work the handles of the sluice gates and to cause the water to cascade into the locks, then to watch while the barge rose, as if by magic, until it reached the level again and they travelled along the next stretch of snow-covered countryside.

On reaching their destination, the bargemen had said that Liam had earned his keep, and they had all gone to a nearby eating-house once the barge had been moored. Liam ate a big meal of Irish stew, followed by apple dumplings, and when he returned to his makeshift bed he felt warm, full and ready for sleep.

His mind drifted to his family, and he hoped that Ma wasn't too worried about him, and that Da had enough to eat in prison and wasn't cold on a wintry night like this. Thinking about them made him more determined than ever, and he swore to himself that he would get to Aunt Molly's tomorrow, no matter what the weather conditions. Normally thoughts like that would have kept keep him awake, but tonight he felt exhausted after what had been an action-packed day. His neck, shoulder and hip still felt sore from when he had jumped off the train, but the slight rocking of the barge and the gentle lapping of the water soothed him, and soon he drifted off to sleep, dreaming of trains and barges and his aunt's farmhouse, miles away across seemingly endless snow-covered fields.

Chapter 20

Nora knew that she mustn't make her mother suspicious this morning, and she was careful to hide her nervousness as she crossed the drawing room, pretending to leave for the Mansion House concert. In reality, her heart was pounding from the huge deception involved in travelling secretly to Hazelwood Farm near Ballinacargy.

'I'll see you this evening, Mummy,' she said.

'Yes, good luck with the concert, dear.'

'Thanks.'

'And I'm sorry it clashed with David's school bazaar, but you do understand, I'd promised to help run it?'

'It's fine,' said Nora. 'There'll be other concerts.'

'If it's a thing I can get away early, I'll try to make it to the Mansion House.'

Nora's blood ran cold. 'No. No, there's no need, Mummy,' she answered quickly.

Her mother looked at her, and Nora feared that she might have over-reacted.

'Really,' she added more casually, 'it's fine. There's no

point having you rushing to get into town.' Nora found herself holding her breath as she waited for her mother's response.

Her mother looked at her again, then shrugged. 'You're right, dear, it probably would be rather rushed. But I'll definitely make the next one.'

'Grand.'

'And you do understand that Daddy can't avoid his Federation meeting?'

'Of course. And please, Mummy, even if his meeting ends a bit early, tell him not to worry about getting in – I know he has lots of stuff going on.'

'All right, dear. Make sure you keep your scarf on to protect your throat. And sing well.'

'I'll try,' said Nora, then she kissed her mother's cheek. 'Bye, Mummy.'

Hiding her relief, Nora quickly exited the drawing room. She put on her hat, scarf and gloves, crossed the hall, picked up her bag and went out the front door. She was hit by a gust of cold morning air, and as she descended the snow-covered steps she realised that the fog that she had seen on first getting up was now a little thicker.

She headed for her tram stop, hoping that the fog wouldn't affect her rail journey, but she decided to stay positive, and told herself that unless the weather in the midlands got extremely bad it shouldn't stop the trains.

Nora waited until she was out of sight of her home, then

she accelerated, running along the pavements, her feet pushing down the crisp snow with a satisfying crunch. She wanted to reach Broadstone Station as quickly as possible, knowing that if she were to get to Westmeath and back in one day it was important to catch the earliest possible train.

She had explained her early departure by telling her mother that Brother Raymond had called a final rehearsal this morning, with the choir scheduled to perform in the Mansion House in the afternoon. Fortunately, her mother had accepted this without question, and Nora's good fortune continued now when, on rounding the corner, she saw a tram approaching. She hailed the driver, then took the tram into the city centre. She got off at the top of Parnell Square and continued on foot towards the railway station via the Black Church and Western Way. This was an area of the city near to where Liam lived, and as she made her way along the foggy, snow-covered streets she was struck again by how lucky she was to live in Leeson Park, instead of in the cramped-looking cottages or the run-down and freezing tenements that she passed.

Walking briskly, she reached the station in a few minutes and entered the main concourse. To her relief it was busy, with plenty of passengers bustling about. Despite the foggy weather the trains must be running. She had planned her next move carefully, and with the money she had taken from her piggy bank in her pocket, she confidently approached the ticket desk. Her only fear was that questions might be asked of a child travelling alone. But she reasoned that with her well-cut clothes, middle-class accent and assured manner she should be able to persuade the ticket clerk that everything was in order – and if need be she had a story ready about being met by a fictitious uncle in Mullingar.

As it was, the bored-looking clerk asked her nothing except her destination, and if he felt that it was unusual for a young girl to travel alone he kept his thoughts to himself. Pleased that things had gone smoothly, and that her money had been more than enough to pay the fare, Nora made her way to the platforms. There was a train leaving for Sligo in five minutes which would stop at Mullingar on the way, and she quickly headed for its carriages.

She already felt guilty about all the lies she had told at home and, not wanting to have to tell any more lies to inquisitive passengers, Nora deliberately went to the carriage furthest down the platform. She stepped on board and saw two middle-aged men with briefcases sitting in the centre of the carriage. *They'd probably be too involved in their business to wonder about a girl travelling alone.* At the far end of the carriage there was a couple, a heavily-built man in his mid-twenties and a woman who, from the possessive way she had her arm wound through his, was obviously the man's sweetheart. *No interference from them either*, thought Nora, then she made her way to the front of the carriage and took a window seat.

She looked out the window, eager to be on her way. She was really looking forward to meeting up with Liam and could hardly wait to see the surprise on his face when she turned up. But still, she reminded herself, this wasn't just an adventure; Liam's family was badly in need of the food, and if Nora's parents found out what she was up to she would be severely punished. Even so, it was hard to suppress a thrill at the daring of what she was doing.

Her thoughts were cut short by the blast of a whistle. The carriage shuddered slightly, and the images of passengers on other platforms began to glide past Nora's gaze, then the train pulled out of the station and began to pick up speed.

※　　※　　※

Liam didn't want to admit to himself that he could be lost. The fog had become steadily worse, and yesterday's snow had covered possible landmarks in an all-enveloping blanket of white, making it hard to keep his bearings. He had been walking for several hours now but at the last two crossroads he had been uncertain of which direction to take. There had been no other travellers on the route and he had seen no roadside cottages at which he could seek directions to Ballinacargy since leaving the crossroads.

He had started out later than he had intended, having slept through until nine o'clock this morning when the bargemen had finally woken him. Although the men had acted out of kindness in letting him sleep, he would have preferred an early start for Aunt Molly's farm. Instead, his da's old friend, Tim Morrissey, had insisted that he have porridge, and tea and bread and butter, to set him up for his onward journey.

It had been after half past nine before he had finally said his farewells and thanked the bargemen for all their kindnesses, then he had set off from the harbour, following Tim's directions for the road to Ballinacargy.

Now he picked his way along snow-covered roads and, although there had been no fresh falls of snow, it was still cold, slow progress as he wound his way through the foggy countryside.

A ruined cottage appeared out of the mist and he came to a stop, wondering what he should do. If he had taken a wrong turn at the crossroads then continuing on would take him further from his destination, wasting precious time and energy. The other choice was to shelter and rest inside the cottage and hope that a fellow traveller would eventually pass, from whom he could get directions. But since leaving the outskirts of Mullingar he had encountered no one else, and he reasoned that nobody would set out on a journey today unless he really had to. Better to push on and hope that he was on the right road.

He breathed out wearily, his breath hanging like a small white cloud in the frozen air, then he set off again, hoping he had made the right decision.

✳ ✳ ✳

Nora stepped briskly from the train the moment it stopped in Mullingar station. She spotted the exit sign and moved quickly, wanting to be out of the building before the other passengers. She didn't know how many carts might be for hire outside the station and she wanted to be first in line, in order to get to Liam's aunt's house as soon as possible. The fog was worse now than when she had left Dublin, and she hoped that the cab drivers who normally plied for business outside train stations wouldn't have stayed at home because of the bad weather.

Carrying nothing but her empty sports bag, Nora had the advantage over most of her fellow passengers, and she was first through the exit door and out into the chill morning air. She braced herself against the cold, then looked about. The snow on the ground here was discoloured and slushy in parts, and there was a big fog-enshrouded area directly in front of her that looked like the marshalling yards for goods trains. To her relief, there was a line of waiting carts, their drivers wrapped up heavily against the cold and the horses standing patiently between the shafts, their occasional whinnies sending plumes of breath into the icy air.

Nora moved to the first man in line.

'I'd like to hire your cab, please,' she said.

'Would you now?' answered the man, looking at her

inquisitively. He had a thin face and a prominent nose, and his head and ears were covered by an ancient-looking woollen cap. There was something weasel-like and off-putting about him, Nora thought, but she determined not to be intimidated and looked him in the eye.

'I've to meet up with my friend. He's staying at Hazelwood Farm near Ballinacargy. Do you know it?'

'I do. That's a fair distance.'

'Can you take me there?'

'Who's paying?

'I am.'

'You're travelling alone?'

'Just till I meet my friend.'

The man seemed to think about this, then he looked at Nora.

'I'd need to see the money before we go.'

'That's all right. On one condition.'

The man looked irritated. 'Since when do girleens like you make conditions?'

Nora held his gaze. Some instinct told her that it would be important to keep the upper hand here. She knew how her mother would respond, and copying her, she spoke as calmly and with as much assurance as she could muster.

'I'm making a condition seeing as I'm the one paying.'

The man looked her in the eye, as though gauging her, then he nodded. 'All right, what is it?'

'I'll show you the money before we leave. But you have to tell me exactly what it will cost – also before we leave.'

The man shook his head. 'I don't know how long it will take me to get there. I've to charge you for my time.'

Nora knew that if she agreed to this there could be trouble later, so she shook her head. 'No. I need to know now what it will cost me.'

The man said nothing, and Nora grew impatient.

'If you don't want to take me I'll go to someone else,' she said.

'All right. I'll do it for a shilling,' the man said.

Nora raised an eyebrow. 'That's more than I expected.'

'Maybe you'd like me to take you for nothing?'

'I can afford eight pence,' said Nora.

The man breathed out in disgust, then looked at her and sighed as if in resignation. 'I'll do it for ten pence, and that's as low as I can go.'

Nora thought that ten pence wasn't too bad, but the man's attitude had been unpleasant from the start, and something in her wanted to best him. 'Nine pence is the best I can do.' She opened her purse and took out a three penny bit and a sixpence. 'That's to show I have it. I'll give you three now and the other six when we get to the farm. All right?'

The man hesitated, then held out his hand for the three pence. 'Right.'

Nora gave him the money, and he dismounted, pulled

down the step and helped her into the back of the cart. He indicated a heavy blanket for Nora to wrap around herself, then without another word, he remounted the cab.

Pleased with her bargaining skills, Nora enveloped herself in the heavy blanket, then she sat back in the cart as the driver cracked his whip and they made for the station exit.

Liam decided that he needed to stop. He had turned another bend and all he could see ahead of him were foggy, snow-covered fields on both sides of the road. He was cold, tired and hungry, so he crossed to a low stone wall and sat on its uneven surface. The wall felt hard and icy, but it was a relief to take the weight off his feet. He reached into his coat pocket and withdrew the sandwiches, wrapped in grease-proof paper, that Tim Morrissey had given him before he left Mullingar. The thick, chewy, buttered slices of loaf bread were filled with home-made blackberry jam and they were a treat that Liam had been saving for when he really needed it.

The full, warm feeling he had experienced on finishing breakfast had long since worn off, and now Liam ate the sandwiches hungrily, washing them down with milk from a small rinsed-out whiskey bottle that Tim had given him.

The food lifted his sprits a little and he shifted on the wall, trying to get more comfortable as he considered his situation. He still wasn't sure if he was on the right road for Ballinacargy.

The only roadside cottage that he had seen in a long time had had no smoke rising from its chimney, and when he had knocked on the door there had been no answer. If he was travelling in the right direction he should reach Aunt Molly's in the next hour or two, but if he had gone astray the situation was worrying. The light was going to go very early in these conditions, and unless the fog lifted he might not be able to locate a farmhouse where he could appeal for help.

He had read stories where people sometimes slept in haystacks, but this was the wrong time of the year for that. More worryingly, in a boys' adventure novel that he had enjoyed recently one of the characters had been stranded during a Canadian winter, and had fallen asleep, exhausted, in a ditch – with fatal results.

It needn't come to that, though. If the worst came to the worst he should be able to retrace his steps and seek refuge in a small townland that he had passed through some time after leaving Mullingar this morning. But that would mean another day lost in his bid to get the food for his family.

He considered his options for a moment, then rose from the wall, wiped the jam from his lips and drained the bottle of milk. Then he stretched his limbs, wrapped his coat tightly around himself and started off again on what he hoped was the Ballinacargy road.

Nora stamped her feet on the floor of the jolting cart, trying to keep warm as they passed through the wintry landscape. After travelling through the outskirts of Mullingar it had become a blur of snow-covered, foggy fields and ditches, and she had lost track of time as they had trundled through the silent countryside. She was dressed in her warmest clothes and had wrapped the coarse woollen blanket provided by the driver tightly around herself, but still her face, hands and feet felt cold.

Nora shifted in her seat, easing her cramped muscles, then she got a shock on seeing a ghostly figure ahead of them in the mist. It was the first person she had seen since they had left Mullingar, but no sooner had she caught a glimpse of the figure than it disappeared again into the fog where the road rounded a bend.

The cart travelled on, and Nora sat upright now, the cold temporarily forgotten as she looked ahead while waiting to overtake the walker. The cart rounded the bend, and Nora could just about make out the figure through the fog. He had stopped, presumably on hearing the sound of the approaching vehicle. The person turned around, and as the cart drew near Nora saw to her amazement that it was Liam.

'Stop! Stop the cart!' cried Nora, rising from her seat even as the driver called out 'whoa' and pulled on the reins.

Nora could see the look of shock on Liam's face, then she quickly climbed over the edge of the cart and jumped to the ground. 'Liam!' she cried, running across the snowy road towards him.

'Nora?'

Nora reached him and without stopping to think she threw her arms around him and hugged him. Even though they were good friends she had never hugged him before, but somehow it seemed the right thing to do now. His face felt even icier than her own, and she drew back and looked at him.

'You're freezing!'

'I'm fine, but I … I can't believe you're here!'

'I know you told me not to, but I had to help. You're not angry, are you?'

'No! No, I'm delighted. I just … I can't believe you've come all this way – and found me out here.'

'Well, it is the road to Ballinacargy.'

'Is it? I wasn't sure if I was lost or not.'

Nora turned to the driver. 'We are definitely on the road to Ballinacargy, aren't we?'

He nodded curtly. 'About a mile, mile-and-a-half to go.'

'Thank God for that,' said Liam.

'How come it's taken you so long to get here?'

'I had a few problems – you won't believe the adventures I've had, Nora.'

'Yeah?'

'I've been sleeping on boats and everything. But what about you? How did you get away?'

'They all think I'm singing at the Mansion House.'

'How long are we going to stop here?' the driver complained.

'Not long,' answered Nora, then she turned back to her friend. 'Do you want to hop up on the cart, and we can catch up on everything?'

Liam looked at her and grinned. 'Sounds good.'

Nora smiled back at him, then they both crossed to the cart, ignored the grumpy face of the driver, and climbed eagerly aboard.

※　※　※

Liam felt a sinking feeling when he saw that up ahead the main gate to the farm was closed. He had been delighted by Nora's surprise appearance and the knowledge that he hadn't been lost after all. That and knowing that he had a friend to help him get the supplies back to Dublin had lifted a weight from his shoulders.

They had chatted excitedly about their mutual adventures, and the time passed quickly, but now Liam was worried. When he had stayed on the farm during summer holidays the main gate had always been left open. It would be a disaster if, after all his efforts, Aunt Molly turned out not to be here.

The cart came to a halt, and the cranky cab driver immediately turned around and held his hand out to Nora.

'Right, the other sixpence please,' he said.

'OK,' answered Nora, rising stiffly and unwrapping the blanket to get at her purse.

While she did so Liam unwrapped the spare blanket that the driver had give him and looked again at the closed gate.

'All right, Liam?' asked Nora.

'Yes, it's just I've never seen the gate shut before. I hope they're here.'

'If there's no one there I can bring you back to Mullingar,' said the cabman as he took the money from Nora. 'Provided you have another nine pence.'

'You have to go back anyway,' she said.

'Doesn't mean I'll bring you for nothing. It's another nine pence if you want to go back.'

'Forget it!' said Liam, jumping down onto the frozen ground and facing the driver. 'Even if they're not here, we'll sort out something. We're not paying you twice.'

'Suit yourself,' said the man, then he looked down at Nora as she got off the cart. 'Are you sure about this? I'll wait a minute if you want to check.'

Nora turned around and looked enquiringly at Liam.

He shook his head at once. Money was far too precious to squander like that, he reckoned. And besides, he wasn't going back empty-handed, even if Aunt Molly wasn't at home. He turned back to the driver. 'Thanks for the offer, mister, but you're grand. Safe journey,' he added with a hint of sarcasm.

The driver looked coldly at him, then he cracked his whip,

turned the cart around and headed back towards Mullingar without another word.

Now that he had burned his bridges, Liam felt a stab of anxiety, but Nora turned to him and smiled.

'Well done. I really didn't like that man,' she said. 'And I was thinking, Liam. You were probably only here in the summer, right?'

'Yes.'

'Maybe they close the gate in the winter. To keep the animals from wandering out in weather like this.'

Liam nodded. 'Maybe. Let's head up the drive and find out.'

Chapter 21

Nora felt the pain throbbing through her toes. But it was a pleasurable pain like you got when your hands turned purple from throwing snowballs and then you heated them at a fire. Nora's feet were thawing out now in front of a blazing turf fire and she sat forward in her chair, revelling in the heat of the farmhouse kitchen.

Liam's aunt Molly was bustling about the room, organising food, drink and dry clothes for Liam, whose outer garments had become damp from hours of exposure to the freezing fog. Nora had taken at once to Molly, who had been shocked to find her frozen-looking nephew on her doorstep. Quickly recovering, she had then made a great fuss, ushering Liam and Nora into the warmth of the kitchen and accepting Nora as she would a niece, on hearing that she was Liam's friend who had come all the way from Dublin to help bring back the food supplies.

Molly was a pretty woman with curly brown hair and bright blue eyes like Liam's, and although she was of slight build she seemed to have boundless energy. She would have needed it, too, to look after three young children and run the farm single-handedly when her husband Mattie was away from home – as he often was, due to his work as a drover.

'It's an awful shame Mattie's not here,' Molly said now. 'He could have met ye at the station.'

'Not to worry,' said Liam, 'we got here in the end.'

'Looking like a couple of frozen mice!' said Molly, then she quickly turned to Nora. 'No offence, Nora. You're very well turned out, lovely outfit,' she said indicating Nora's clothes approvingly. 'But you both could have caught your death of cold.'

'Well, we're getting nice and warm now,' answered Nora, 'so it worked out OK.'

'Sure God is good,' said Molly. 'And so is your mother, Nora. It was very decent of her to give you the train fare to come down and help Liam.'

'Yes, well, she … she believes in doing right.' Nora caught Liam's eye, and seeing him trying to hold back a smile, she quickly looked away. She felt bad about misleading Molly, but she and Liam had decided that it would be best not to reveal that Nora was here unbeknownst to her family.

She thought about her family now while Molly laid places at the table and Liam chatted with his shy country cousins, a little boy of about four, called Michael, and the six year-old twins, Ellen and Bridget.

There was going to be terrible trouble with Mummy, Nora

knew, because it was obvious that they weren't going to get back to Dublin tonight. Liam's clothes had to be dried out, Molly was insistent that they needed a hot meal, the food supplies had to be parcelled up, and in the present weather conditions it wasn't possible to set up transport to Mullingar easily, which meant that they weren't going to make the Dublin train.

Mary would deliver the letter, so at least her parents would know where she had gone. But still there would be hell to pay. She had lied about what she was doing, she had disobeyed her mother in remaining friends with Liam, she had put herself at risk travelling unescorted to a place she didn't know. And she had – as her parents would see it – betrayed her class in the battle between employers and workers. But in spite of everything, Nora had no regrets. She had done what she thought was right and she would take the consequences.

She wiggled her toes now, the feeling coming back into them. She had originally been fairly hopeful that she could make the trip to Ballinacargy and back on the same day, but since she couldn't, there was no point fretting. The important thing now was to get the precious supplies back to Dublin – otherwise everything would have been in vain.

She shifted again in her chair, savouring the heat of the big turf fire, then she thought about Liam's plan for tomorrow and prayed that it would all work out.

* * *

The only light in the darkened kitchen was the dim red glow from the embers of the turf fire. Everyone except Liam was gone up to bed, and with Nora installed in the only spare bedroom, Molly had set up a mattress and blankets for him in front of the kitchen fire. It was the second night in a row that he had slept in a makeshift bed, but Liam had no complaints. He knew that it was freezing hard outside, but the kitchen was still warm, and as he stretched out under the comforting weight of the blankets he felt a delightful cosiness.

Molly had insisted that after getting cold and damp from his long walk he needed a hot bath, and she had dried his wet clothes at the fire while Liam luxuriated in a tin bath that Molly had set up in the scullery and then filled with kettles of hot water.

The bath, followed by a big meal of bacon and cabbage, had made Liam feel full and contented, and he envied his country cousins, who, although they might not have much money, were never going to go hungry while living on the farm.

All the more reason, Liam knew, why he had to get the food supplies back to his own family in Dublin. But that was a challenge for tomorrow, and tonight he felt warm, and dry and full.

Even sleeping on the kitchen floor with the soothing red glow of the fire and the scent of turf was an enjoyable novelty

– Nora had said it reminded her of a scene from an adventure book, and Liam knew what she meant.

Thinking of Nora, he reflected again on what a good friend she was. His father had always claimed that rich people were pampered and weak, but for once Da was wrong. Nora was strong and brave even though she was rich. And working people weren't always kind and decent, Liam thought, remembering the ticket collector on the train and the money-grasping cab driver. But of course other people like the bargemen more than made up for that. The trip to Ballinacargy had been an eye-opener, though, and the more he looked back over his adventures the more he realised that things rarely turned out as you thought they would. What should he expect tomorrow then, when he tried to get the supplies back to Dublin? Whatever he planned, he sensed that things would happen in ways he couldn't anticipate. *So why worry now?* he thought. Instead he breathed in the aroma of warm turf, curled up even more under the blankets and let his eyes lazily close for sleep.

Chapter 22

The argument was over now, and as Nora prepared to return to Dublin she knew that she had been right to challenge Liam.

She had risen early to a crisp winter's morning, with yesterday's fog and snow replaced by bright sunshine. It had still been really cold as Nora dressed, and the early morning sunlight sparkled on the frosty farmyard implements, while the surrounding countryside had looked magical as the sun cast a yellow glow on the snow-covered fields.

Liam had risen early also, and he had drawn Nora aside in the farmyard, wanting to talk to her out of earshot of Molly.

'There's something I don't want Molly to know,' he had said.

Nora looked at him with interest. 'What?'

'She's given me whatever money she can spare,' said Liam. 'As a loan to Da and Ma,' he added hastily.

'And what do you not want her to know?'

'That I won't be wasting any of it paying a train fare. Every penny counts back in Dublin.'

'But mightn't you be caught again by the guard if you've no ticket?'

'No,' answered Liam. 'My mistake last time was travelling in the passenger carriage. This time I'll sneak into a goods wagon in Mullingar.'

'How do you know there'll be a goods wagon attached?'

'There was the last time, so there'll probably be again.'

'OK, I won't say anything to Molly.'

'Thanks, Nora.'

'And I'll do the same. Then we can save my fare as well.'

Liam immediately shook his head. 'No.'

'Why not?'

'It's enough that you came all the way down here,' he said. 'I don't want you getting into any more trouble.'

'I won't if we're not caught,' answered Nora. 'And you're not planning on getting caught, are you?'

'No. But still.'

'But still, what?'

'If you pay your fare and take half the food, we could be sure of at least that much getting to Dublin,' explained Liam.

'And if I travel with you we could get *all* the food to Dublin and add my fare to what Molly gave. You said yourself that every penny counts.'

Nora could tell that Liam saw the logic of this, but he still hesitated.

'I can't be taking more money off you,' he said.

'For goodness sake, Liam! We're friends, we're in this together. Call it a loan, the same as the money from Molly.'

Nora could see that Liam's resistance was weakening and she decided to go for broke. 'Anyway,' she said, 'I'm not *asking* if I can hide in the goods carriage. I'm *telling* you that I'm doing it.'

Liam looked at her a moment and she thought that she had gone too far. Instead he suddenly grinned.

'You're mad,' he said, 'but you're sound as a pound!'

That had been a couple of hours ago and since then Molly had served a hearty breakfast of porridge, boiled eggs and brown bread, having first gone to a neighbouring farm to discuss transport to Mullingar. She had been gone for half an hour, then had returned, smiling. The improved weather would make travel easier, and a neighbouring farmer, Joe Pat Foley, would take Liam and Nora to town in his cart.

Molly had then parcelled the foodstuffs, consisting of flour, oatmeal, butter, home-made bread, sugar and cuts of bacon and mutton. She had also carefully wrapped about twenty eggs in cardboard, then divided the heavy load between Nora's sports bag and a battered case that she had given to Liam.

Now the entire group stood in the slush-covered farmyard, their breath rising in clouds in the wintry air. Joe Pat Foley, a kindly-looking man with bushy red whiskers, loaded the luggage into his cart, between whose shafts stood a sturdy grey mare. Liam's cousins had come out to see them off, their initial shyness of yesterday gone as they excitedly said their goodbyes to Liam and Nora.

Molly herself then stepped forward, tears in her eyes even as she smiled and hugged Liam.

'Tell your ma I'm praying for her, Liam. And I said a novena that they'd let Billy out soon. Tell her that, she knows I have a great leg of Saint Francis!'

'I will,' answered Liam. 'And thanks for everything, you were brilliant.'

'Will you go along outta that,' answered Molly, then she turned to Nora. 'Come here, love, and give me a hug,' she said.

Nora hugged her, struck by the thought that her mother would be slow to hug someone she had known for less than twenty-four hours. The thought of home made her briefly anxious about what lay ahead, but Nora determinedly put her worries from her mind. She smiled at Molly when they finished hugging and extended her hand as she had been taught. 'Thank you so much for all your hospitality, Mrs Halligan,' she said.

'You're more than welcome, love,' replied Molly, then she turned to Liam and made a gesture of appreciation towards Nora. 'Beautiful manners.'

'Whenever you're ready!' cried Joe Pat, climbing up into the driver's seat of the cart.

There was a final flurry of goodbyes, and Nora and Liam climbed aboard.

'Yup,' cried Joe Pat, cracking his whip, then the grey moved off and they rattled across the farmyard.

Nora waved farewell until all of Liam's relations were out of sight, then she settled back in the cart as they started the long and unpredictable journey home.

✳   ✳   ✳

Liam walked with the confident air of someone going about his lawful business as he made his way back towards Nora's hiding place. Joe Pat had dropped them off in Mullingar, and the return journey through a beautiful, snow-covered and sunlit landscape had been in strong contrast to the foggy and confusing route that Liam had travelled only yesterday.

They had thanked Joe Pat, then made their way to the canal bank and found a thickly wooded area nearby, where Nora had hidden from view with the food while Liam did a reconnaissance at the train station.

Being a Sunday morning, Mullingar was busy, and despite the cold weather lots of people were attending church services. Liam felt that it was important not to draw attention by skulking around or looking suspicious, which was why he strode along now with the air of a boy with a definite purpose. He reached the wooded area and cut in through the snow-laden trees to reach a small clearing where Nora was sitting on his upturned case. She rose and looked at him enquiringly.

'Well?'

'Good news. There are plenty of people out and about – though we'll still need to be very careful in the station.'

'Right.'

'And there's a train leaving for Dublin in half an hour, with two goods carriages.'

'Brilliant,' said Nora.

'Yeah. They're packing them with parcels right now. If we time it properly, we should be able to slip on board when they have the parcels stowed, but before the train pulls out.'

'Right.'

'There's one other thing though, Nora, and it's important.'

'What?'

'When it comes to getting on, I go first. If I'm caught, you walk away. Pretend you don't know me, OK?'

Liam could see that Nora was hesitant, and he looked at her appealingly. 'Please. There's no point in you getting into trouble as well.'

'I know, but–'

'No buts, Nora, I really mean it. If you're not caught you can still buy a ticket, get to Dublin and deliver the food to my ma.'

Liam could see that Nora recognised the sense of this, and he didn't need to emphasise how important it was to get at least some of the food to his mother.

'Promise me that's what you'll do if I'm caught,' he said.

Nora looked him in the eye, then nodded slowly. 'You have my word.'

'Thanks, Nora. So, are you ready to try it?'

'Absolutely.'

'OK. Let's go.'

Chapter 23

This was the moment of maximum danger. Nora was hiding with Liam behind a stack of cardboard boxes in one of the two guard's vans used for transporting light goods, and if they were discovered now it would be obvious they were stowaways.

The approach to the station had been nerve-racking, but Nora had followed Liam's advice and had strolled along as though she was just another passenger. The sports bag packed with food was heavy, but Nora had disguised the fact by concentrating on carrying it as though it was just a normal weight.

They hadn't entered the station through the main passenger hall, instead turning in through the marshalling yards, ready if anyone challenged them to offer the excuse that they weren't locals and had taken a wrong turn. But no one had come near them and, with most of the station activity taking place at the platform towards the front of the train, they had managed to climb quickly into one of the open guard's vans at the rear.

Liam's reconnaissance had paid off – the parcels were already loaded on board – and Nora reckoned that the train must be almost due to leave now. She found herself becoming more anxious. Supposing someone did an inspection to make sure all the boxes were sufficiently secure? Or suppose one of the railway men chose to travel back to Dublin in the guard's van? Her thoughts were suddenly disturbed by a wheezing sound at the entrance to the carriage. Nora held her breath as she heard a man climbing on board. She strained her ears for any clue to what was going on, then her heart began pounding on hearing the wheezing getting louder as the man headed her way.

Liam urgently signalled to Nora not to make a sound. The laboured breathing drew closer, and both of them stood stock still. The man must be only two or three feet away now, moving slowly. Liam bit his lip nervously, praying that the stranger would stop before discovering their hiding place. Just when he seemed to be almost upon them, the man grunted, then there was a thud and Liam realised that he had lowered whatever he had been carrying to the floor of the carriage.

You've done what you came for, Liam thought, *now turn around and go away.* Instead the wheezing continued, and Liam caught sight of Nora making a grimace. He looked questioningly at her and saw that she was about to sneeze. She had sneezed several times on the journey back through the wintry countryside, but another one now would be disastrous. Liam urgently mimicked pinching her nose to hold in the sneeze, and Nora quickly did as Liam had indicated, making only a small involuntary sound as the sneeze shook her.

Despite the cold, Liam could feel a bead of sweat forming on his brow as he waited to see if the wheezing man had heard. He listened for what seemed like an eternity, but was probably only a second or two, and then he heard the man move away, followed by a low groan suggesting that he had lowered himself from the carriage down to the platform.

Liam looked at Nora, and she breathed out and smiled in nervous relief. He smiled in return, but neither of them spoke. Suddenly there was a sound of squeaky rollers rumbling and the carriage began to darken as the door of the carriage was pulled across. Liam listened intently, knowing that the next few seconds were critically important. If the door was simply closed, then he could slide it open when the train reached Dublin. If it was locked from the outside they would be trapped inside until the lever was released.

The door slammed shut and Liam strained anxiously, hoping not to hear the fall of the lock. He stood there, his jaws gripped tight with tension, then he slowly breathed out, realising that the lever hadn't been applied. He turned to Nora and gave her a thumbs-up sign, and she smiled broadly and raised her thumb in return.

The air was pierced by a loud whistle, and a couple of seconds later the carriage jolted and began to move slowly forward. Liam mopped his forehead and leaned back against the boxes behind him, hugely relieved that they were finally leaving Mullingar. They weren't safe yet, far from it. But they *were* on a train heading for Broadstone, and they had the precious food supplies. There would be more challenges to come, he had no doubt, but meanwhile they could relax for a little while before deciding their tactics for when the train arrived in Dublin.

❋   ❋   ❋

Nora got up nervously from her makeshift seat of cardboard boxes as the train pulled into the terminus at Broadstone. The interior of the guard's van was gloomy with the door closed, but she could still see the tension on Liam's face. He rose too as the train slowed down and, with no hint of his usual mischievous expression, he held out his hand.

'Thanks for everything, Nora,' he said, 'you've been … you've just been the best.'

'I wouldn't have missed it for anything.'

'You're sure you want to go ahead with your plan?'

'Certain,' answered Nora.

They had spent half of the journey from Mullingar to

Dublin discussing the best approach to getting out of Broadstone station undetected. With Liam about to be weighed down by food, they had agreed that it would be too risky for him to try to exit through the busy marshalling yards, but right now Nora didn't want to think any more about her own plan in case she lost her nerve.

'OK,' said Liam, 'let's be ready to get off once it stops.'

They both moved the bags of food to the door, then stood at the ready. Nora could hear the groaning sound of brakes being applied and steam released, then the train finally came to a halt.

Liam grasped the door handle at once and heaved. Nothing happened, and Nora felt a flutter of panic. Liam hauled again, and this time the door slowly moved a couple of feet, rumbling sideways and allowing light and smoky station air into the carriage.

As agreed, Nora took a quick look out, then jumped down first onto the platform. All along the platform train doors were being opened and passengers were alighting, but Nora's concern was for station staff. So far it seemed as though she hadn't been noticed

She called back to Liam. 'All clear!'

Liam swung the sports bag full of supplies out the door and Nora swiftly took it, followed by Liam's battered suitcase. Liam followed instantly, jumping down onto the platform and immediately taking up the case.

Nora hoisted the sports bag and began walking towards the front of the train and the ticket barrier. Trying to be casual, she glanced about her as she walked. She half expected a hand on her shoulder or a cry from some railway official, but with throngs of people getting off the train and moving towards the exit no one appeared to have spotted their descent from the goods wagon.

One problem solved, thought Nora, but the tricky part was still to come. They shuffled forward with all the other travellers to the gate where a portly official was collecting the tickets of the arriving passengers. The queue was moving briskly and when they were several places from the front Nora tapped Liam's leg. He reached out his free hand and surreptitiously gripped the straps of her sports bag, taking it from her. They had made sure not to chat or in any way acknowledge each other, and Nora moved one space ahead of Liam as though travelling alone.

Now that the moment for action was drawing close she felt her mouth becoming dry, and she swallowed hard. Timing was going to be everything here, and she waited until she was two places away from the ticket collector, then she felt her coat pockets frantically and cried out, 'My money! My money's been stolen!'

Nora could see the ticket collector and lots of the passengers looking at her, and she decided that a little more hysteria was in order. 'All my money! Someone took my purse with all my money!' she cried, her voice quivering with apparent upset.

'You poor thing. Do you live near here?' said a motherly-looking woman who was directly ahead of her in the queue.

'No! What am I going to do?' cried Nora, looking at the ticket collector.

He raised his hand soothingly.

'It'll be all right, don't get yourself upset. Are you meeting your parents?' he asked.

'I was … I was supposed to get a cab with the money, but now it's all gone,' she sobbed.

There were murmurings of sympathy around her, and the ticket collector tried to console Nora. She began to sob even more, and from the corner of her eye she glimpsed Liam slipping past the distracted ticket collector. Laden down by the combined weight of the sports bag and suitcase he couldn't move quickly, but that was OK, Nora thought, he would draw less attention while moving at a moderate speed.

'How am I going to get home?' wailed Nora, anxious to give Liam as much time as possible to make his way through the station.

'We'll get the police, they'll take you home,' said the ticket collector.

'Or maybe … maybe we could ring my parents?' suggested Nora a little more calmly, now that she realised that Liam was no longer anywhere to be seen. *We've done it*, she thought triumphantly, *we've done it!*

'Tell you what,' said the ticket man. 'Let me finish collecting the tickets and then we'll take you to the station master's office. You can ring your parents from there. All right?'

'Yes, all right,' answered Nora. 'And thank you so much.'

Liam trudged along Western Way, the weight of the sports bag and suitcase making his arms and shoulders ache. The snow on the footpaths here was dirtier and slushier than it had been in Westmeath, and Liam moved carefully, watching out for icy patches. He turned left into the warren of streets that led to his home, his mind racing. Nora's plan had worked to perfection, although he still wasn't entirely happy about leaving her behind while he escaped. But Nora had insisted that it would be a disaster if, after all their efforts to get the food to Dublin, they were both caught at the last moment and quite possibly taken away and arrested. She had pointed out that she was already in trouble with her parents, and it would hardly be any worse if they came to Broadstone to collect her when she pretended that her purse was stolen.

It was hard to argue with her logic – and Liam knew how determined she could be – so eventually he had agreed to her plan. He hoped now that she wouldn't get in too much trouble when her parents heard of all that she had done. He hoped also that his own mother wouldn't be too angry with him for going to Ballinacargy. He had a trump card in the vital bags of food, however, and he was counting on her relief at their delivery to make her overlook everything else. He would also need her to write a note to Brother Kiernan, excusing Liam's absence from school last Friday, and he would have to slip back to the marshalling yards at Broadstone to retrieve his hidden schoolbag.

Wrapped up in his thoughts, Liam had been walking slowly, his head down as he tried to keep the two heavy bags balanced. Now he became aware of a figure in front of him. Liam looked up to see Martin Connolly, the toughest boy in his class and the one who had called him a sissy for singing 'Ave Maria' in the feis.

'Liam,' said Connolly, eyeing the bags curiously.

'Martin,' acknowledged Liam.

The other boy was standing directly in his path, and Liam hesitated, weighing up his options. He didn't want trouble with Connolly, especially not now when he was so close to bringing the food safely home. Liam's arms were already aching, so he opted to put the bags down and try to distract the other boy.

'I couldn't get to school on Friday,' he said. 'Was Killer gunning for me?'

'He asked if anyone knew why you weren't in, but no one did.'

'OK.'

'Where were you?'

'I had to go to my aunt's.'

'Right,' said Connolly as though this finished the topic. He looked at the two bags, then looked at Liam. 'What's in the bags?'

Liam considered for a moment. Could he convince Connolly that all they contained was second-hand clothes? But even old clothes might be something the impoverished Connollys would be keen to get their hands on.

'What's in them?' repeated Connolly.

'Food for my family,' answered Liam. He was suddenly tired of watching his every word. He had gone through too much to get the food to here, and he wasn't going to be timid or apologetic about it. And if Martin Connolly tried to take so much as a crumb, then Liam would fight him, toughest boy in the class or not.

'Where did you get food?' asked Connolly.

'From my aunt down the country.'

There was a pause, and Liam tensed himself, his fists bunched.

Connolly held Liam's gaze, then he looked away. 'Lucky you,' he said resignedly.

Liam looked at him in surprise, and in that moment he saw, not the terror of the school yard, but a beaten, rake-thin boy whose cockiness had been eroded by hunger that possibly bordered on starvation. Liam felt a sudden pity for him and before he knew what he was doing he blurted out, 'Do you want a sandwich?'

Connolly looked at Liam, clearly taken aback by the offer, then he nodded vigorously. 'Yeah.'

Liam took from his coat pocket the last of a large package of ham sandwiches that Aunt Molly had wrapped in grease-proof paper and given to Liam and Nora for the train journey. He handed the sandwich to Connolly who wolfed it down in a matter of seconds.

Liam felt slightly embarrassed by the other boy's public display of hunger, then Connolly looked at him.

'That was ... that was great. Thanks, Liam.'

'You're all right.'

'I'll give you a hand to carry the stuff home.'

'It's OK, I can manage.'

'No, I will. For the sandwich.'

That made sense to Liam. If Martin helped carry the bags, the sandwich might seem a little less like charity and more like a payment.

'All right so. You take the suitcase, I'll take the bag,' said Liam.

They took one piece each and started on their way, treading carefully on the icy pavements, then Connolly turned the corner ahead of Liam. They were entering Liam's street now and he called ahead.

'That's grand now, Martin. I can take it from here.'

Connolly turned to face him. 'I'll carry it in for you,' he said.

'No, that's … that's something I want to do myself.'

'OK,' answered Connolly as though he understood the significance of this for Liam. 'And thanks for the sandwich.'

Liam looked at Connolly, then spontaneously lowered the sports bag and opened the top of it. He took out one of Aunt Molly's loaves of brown bread and offered it to the other boy. 'For your family,' said Liam.

Connolly looked at him almost disbelievingly, then took the loaf.

'I … I won't forget this, Liam. Thanks.' He nodded, then quickly turned and walked away.

Liam watched him go. He felt good, not just because of being able to help someone else, but because, despite all the obstacles he had encountered, he had succeeded in his mission. He allowed himself to savour the idea for a little while, then he took up both bags and walked happily towards his hall door.

✳   ✳   ✳

Nora stood on the steps of Broadstone station, trying to control the butterflies in her stomach. She had been dreading the arrival of her mother and father, but another part of her was anxious to get it over with, knowing that she had to face them at some point.

She had rung from the station master's office a little

earlier, and her father had answered the telephone immediately. He sounded more agitated than Nora had ever heard him, but she had assured him that she was all right and had promised to explain everything when they were reunited.

Nora had thanked the station master for his kindness, and managed to persuade him not to involve the police in the matter of her fictitious stolen purse – she said her father would report the theft. Now she waited at the entrance with a railway man whom the station master had insisted should remain with her until her parents arrived.

Nora's pulse accelerated as she saw the family Ford turning into the slip road leading up to the station entrance.

'These are my parents now,' she said to the railway man. 'Thank you for waiting with me.'

'You're welcome, Miss,' said the man, touching his hat and heading off as the car drew in to the kerb.

Nora could see her mother in the passenger seat, grim-faced and anxious. Her father got out and came round to the front of the car. He saw Nora and, unusually for him, neglected to open the passenger door for his wife, but ran instead towards his daughter.

'We've been worried sick!' he cried. 'Are you really all right?'

'I'm fine, Daddy,' she answered, then without another word her father reached out and hugged her.

Nora hugged him back, pleased that for now he was more

relieved than angry. He stroked her hair, and Nora felt a stab of guilt at how much worry she had caused.

Her father eventually released her, and looking past him, Nora saw that her mother had exited the car and was bearing down on her. Nora felt her earlier butterflies intensifying. Her mother had always been the disciplinarian at home, and this was the moment that Nora had dreaded. She stepped aside from her father and nervously stood her ground. He mother didn't speak, but looked hard at Nora, then ran forward and embraced her.

'Nora, darling. You gave us such a fright.'

Nora had been expecting a blazing row, but to her surprise she saw that there were tears in her mother's eyes.

'I'm sorry, Mummy,' she said, then her mother gripped her more tightly and hugged her. Nora felt the tears forming in her own eyes, and although she knew that later there might be all sorts of trouble, right now she felt relieved and loved, and as a tear rolled down her cheek, she lost herself in her mother's embrace, happy to be safely home again.

Chapter 24

'Liam! It's Liam!' cried Eileen, running forward excitedly as he stepped into the hallway. His other sisters crowded around him, and Liam couldn't help but enjoy their obvious pleasure at his safe return. He looked past them after a moment, to the table where his mother had been sitting, her sewing spread out before her.

She rose now and came towards him. Before she could say anything, Liam indicated the two heavy bags.

'I got the food, Ma,' he said. 'I'm sorry for going behind your back – but we needed it. And I got loads of stuff, it'll really help.'

'Oh, Liam,' cried his mother. 'You're one in a million!'

She hugged him, and Liam smiled and held her close, pleased that she wasn't annoyed at him.

'Aunt Molly was asking for you,' said Liam when his mother finally released him.

'How is she?'

'She's grand. And she said she's going to do a novena to St Francis for Da.'

Ma smiled, but it was a strange smile, as though she were aware of a joke that Liam wasn't in on.

'What is it?' he said.

'She can save her prayers.'

Liam turned around, startled. For there, standing in the bedroom door, was Da. He looked thinner and paler than when he had first been taken to prison, but he still had a twinkle in his eye and he cocked his head sideways and looked at Liam with a crooked grin.

'Do you not have an aul' hug for your da?' he asked.

Liam ran to him and jumped into his arms like he used to do as a small boy. His father hoisted him up in the air and swung him around playfully before gently setting him down again.

'When did you get out, Da?' asked Liam.

'This morning. Your ma's told me what you did, heading off to Westmeath. I'm proud of you, son. Really proud.'

'Thanks, Da. And … and how come they let you out?'

'I think they'd had enough of my company.'

'No really, Da, why?'

'Public opinion, Liam. Every fair-minded person knows this lockout is wrong.'

'And what about Mr Larkin?'

'He's working hard to get the English workers to come in behind us.'

'And will they?'

'I don't know, Liam. The politics are …' Da grimaced. 'It's

complicated, but we'll hope for the best.'

'Right.'

'But we're not going to worry about any of that tonight. Tonight we'll burn whatever coal we have in a blaze. And we'll have lots of food, thanks to you. So we'll be warm, and full, and all together again as a family. Now doesn't that make us luckier than lots of people?'

'It does, Da,' said Liam. He looked around the room at his mother, and his sisters, and Da with his laughing eyes. *He wasn't just luckier than lots of people. He was the luckiest boy in Dublin.*

He smiled at them all, then he bent down and began to open the first of the bags.

'Just wait till I show you what we've got,' he said.

✳ ✳ ✳

Nora folded her letter and placed it in a stamped envelope, then leaned back in her chair and gazed out the window. She was sitting in the drawing room, a log fire roaring in the grate, while outside in the garden the snow was melting and dripping from the branches of the gaunt winter trees.

It was two days now since she had returned from Ballinacargy and, as she had expected, after the first surge of joy and relief had died down, she had been questioned at length. She had been queried about Liam, about Brother Raymond, about the choir, and about all that had happened on her journey to and from Westmeath.

Her parents had not been as angry as they might have been, even when Nora said that despite being sorry for the worry she had caused them, her sympathies still lay with families like Liam's. When, however, she added that she hoped Mr Larkin succeeded in winning an honourable settlement of the lock-out, it had gone down badly, especially with her mother. Nora had stayed polite and respectful, and had explained that her eyes had been opened and this was now her honest, heartfelt view. She knew even as she said it that her parents might bar her from seeing Liam again, seeing him as a bad influence, but she felt that the time for lies was over and that from here on she had to tell the truth, no matter what.

She thought back over all that had happened, then she withdrew her letter from its envelope, wanting to be sure she had covered everything that needed to be said, and she began to read.

Dear Liam,

I hope you are well and that your family is enjoying the food we got from your Aunt Molly. She's a lovely woman, and I really liked her – and especially her brilliant apple tart! Anyway, I hope you didn't get into too much trouble at home, and that your mother let you off when she saw all the food you brought back.

Mummy and Daddy collected me from Broadstone and they were so relieved to find me all right that they hardly gave out to me at all on Sunday night. Since then they've asked me loads of questions, though, and Mummy is annoyed that I went behind her back to be friends with you and that I'm on Mr Larkin's side in the lockout.

The really bad news is that they're taking me out of the choir, and after this letter I'm not allowed have any more contact with you, so I can't write to you again or get letters from you. I tried so hard to argue with them, Liam, but it was no good. Mummy claims that it's not a punishment, but I know it is. She says it's her duty to see that I'm protected from 'influences not in my best interest'. I tried to explain how much I learnt from being your friend and from seeing both sides of the argument about the lockout, but she wouldn't listen.

I'm really sorry they won't let us stay friends, Liam, because you were a great friend and I'll miss you. And no matter what Mummy says, I'll never be sorry we met and I'll remember all the fun we had. And I hope too that Mr Larkin wins out with the lockout, it's only fair that he should, and I'll pray that that happens.

I'm sorry that you and I can't do any more together to help, but we played our part as best we could and that's something I'll always be proud of.

I don't know what else to say, Liam. It's awful that they won't let us stay friends. But Mummy has put her foot down and she made me promise that there'll be no more lies, so I can't go behind her back again. Maybe when we're older and all the strikes and disputes are over we'll meet again. I really hope so. Until then I know I'll think about you, and meanwhile I'll pray for you and your family. Thank you so much for being my friend.

Yours sincerely,
Nora Reynolds.

Nora sat looking at the letter, but she knew that she had said things as well as she could and that there was no point putting off the inevitable. So she placed the letter in the envelope once again, and this time she licked the flap and sealed it. She got up and went to the door, moving out of the warm room and into the hall, where she took her overcoat and scarf from the hat stand. Now that she had made her mind up, she moved quickly, stepping out the hall door and down the steps into the garden.

She walked along Leeson Park, turning into Dartmouth Road and heading for the pillar box at the corner. She felt a strange mix of emotions as she walked along. She was sorry that her time with Liam was at an end, but somehow she wasn't all that surprised. It was as though, deep down, she had always known that sooner or later her mother would put a stop to their friendship.

Still, they had enjoyed their eight months together. They had sung, and laughed and had fun, but Nora had also seen inside Liberty Hall and delivered food parcels to people in need, and in the process had seen the world outside of her own comfortable circle.

And last but not least, Liam had given her the chance to make a stand. On the day that Miss Dillon had been dismissed from the school Nora had sworn that she would do something concrete, something of which her inspirational teacher would approve. And throwing caution to the wind and following Liam to Ballinacargy so his family didn't go hungry was something that Nora would never regret, something she sensed might already have changed her life forever.

She thought of Miss Dillon now, and even though she knew that her former teacher was in England, she imagined her somehow knowing of Nora's actions and being proud of her. It was a nice feeling and it made Nora smile. Then it was time, she knew, to end things. She looked at the letter in her hand, whispered *Bye, Liam* to herself, then slipped the envelope into the pillar box, turned away and started back for home.

EPILOGUE

In January 1914, after over four months of misery and strife, the lockout ended in victory for the employers. It was a limited victory, however, and the lockout came to be seen as a turning point, after which workers were never again treated as badly as they had been before Jim Larkin came to Dublin, and his trade union recovered and went on to become even more powerful.

Nora's father's business was damaged by the lockout, as were lots of other companies, but in time it too recovered, and Mr Reynolds carried on for many years as a successful wine importer, while Nora's mother continued to sit on the boards of numerous charities.

Liam's father was earmarked as a trouble-maker and not taken back at his job when the lockout ended. Unable to find work anywhere in Dublin, he joined the Royal Navy, where his skills as a mechanic were recognised, leading to a success-ful career as a Petty Officer. Liam's mother picked up more work as a dressmaker, and had another child the following year, a baby brother on whom Liam doted, and who was, unsurprisingly, named Jim.

The progressive school in Yorkshire suited Miss Dillon, and less than ten years after her arrival there she was appointed principal.

Brother Raymond's choir – without Nora, but with Liam still a member – went on to win many prizes.

Martin Connolly survived the food shortages of the

lockout, but died later from TB, two weeks after his fifteenth birthday.

Liam trained as a mechanic. When his father finally left the Royal Navy they opened a small garage together, and in time Liam went on to own a number of garages on the north side of Dublin. He no longer had time for choirs, but in the bath he still sang 'Has Anyone Here Seen Kelly?' much to the amusement of his family.

Nora did well in school. She attended University College, Dublin and got an Honours degree in English. Against her mother's wishes, she went to London where she worked successfully as an editor with a large publishing company. At her parents' insistence, she had never told her friends and relatives the true story of Liam and the trip to Ballinacargy. But she still remembered every detail, and one day, when the time was right, she knew she would tell the story of a special friendship. A friendship so strong it reached across the divide …

HISTORICAL NOTE

Although *Across the Divide* is a work of fiction, and Liam and Nora and their families are creations of my imagination, the background to the story is very real and many children of Liam and Nora's age were deeply affected by the severe food shortages and general upheaval of what became known as the Dublin Lockout of 1913.

The tenement living conditions that horrified Nora, with up to seventy people sharing a single toilet, and large numbers of children dying in infancy, were, unfortunately, the everyday reality for many poor people in Dublin.

All the main historical events described in the book really happened, from the baton charge in Sackville Street, (now O'Connell Street, where Jim Larkin's statue can be seen, opposite the GPO) to the tram drivers abandoning their vehicles, to the ships steaming up the Liffey with food for the hungry workers and their families. The food kitchen in Liberty Hall operated as described, and children being sent by their parents to sympathetic families in England were forcibly prevented from leaving the country.

James Larkin's union, the Irish Transport and General

Workers Union [ITGWU], although defeated in the Lock-out, recovered quickly and eventually went on to merge with other unions and become SIPTU, currently the largest trade union in Ireland.

The groups of men who had banded together to protect the striking workers from attacks by the police grew into the Citizen Army, which would go on to take a leading part in the 1916 Rising, under the command of James Connolly, who was executed after the Rising.

All the songs that the characters sing were the actual songs that people loved in 1913 – the pop songs of the era. The tango melodies that Nora and Liam were so keen to hear were part of a genuine musical craze that swept Europe around that time.

The Fr Mathew Hall in Church Street, where *feiseanna* were held over many years, is still standing, but has been converted into an office building.

In the wider world, the Panama Canal, linking the Atlantic and Pacific oceans, had its final section cleared by a controlled explosion, exactly as described.

In 1913, Prime Minister Asquith of Britain was lobbied, unsuccessfully, to build a tunnel linking England and France, and it wasn't until 1994 that the Channel Tunnel was opened. The *Eurostar* high speed train that runs through the tunnel can now bring passengers from London to Paris in less than two hours, thirty minutes.

Sir Almroth Wright's book *The Unexpurgated Case against Woman Suffrage*, which Nora tried to argue against, was a real publication that attacked the ideas of the Suffragette movement. The suffragettes were criticised, arrested, sent to jail and even force-fed during hunger strikes. Eventually their determination paid off, however, and in 1918 women were granted the vote.

The barge on which Liam travelled was of a type used extensively in Ireland to transport goods such as barley, coal, turf and beer. Aunt Molly's Hazelwood Farm is imaginary, but Ballinacargy is a real village, and in the past it was an important halting point on the Royal Canal.

You can still enjoy a night's entertainment at the Gaiety Theatre, just as Nora did. Although now closed, Bewleys Café in Westmoreland Street, where Liam, Nora and the choir members had their coffee and cakes, was a real place, as are Skerries, Torquay, Leeson Park and the other locations that feature in the story.

Brian Gallagher
Dublin, 2010.

If you liked *Across the Divide*, you'll enjoy these other historical fiction titles from **The O'Brien Press:**

A Boy. A Girl.
A Nation Torn Apart.

Taking
Sides

Brian Gallagher

TAKING SIDES
Brian Gallagher

Annie Reilly is delighted when she wins a scholarship to Eccles Street School. There she makes friends with Susie O'Neill and through her, Peter Scanlon. But Civil War is looming and Peter becomes involved with the rebels, putting not just himself, but Annie and her father in danger. Will Peter betray his cause to save Annie, and will she ever be able to trust him again?

A story of friendship, danger and divided loyalties, set against the background of the Civil War.

THE YOUNG REBELS
Morgan Llywelyn

John Joe and Roger are pupils at Padraic Pearse's famous school, St Enda's. The Easter Rising is their chance to fight for Ireland's freedom, and although they are too young to take part, they become caught up in the dramatic events of the Rebellion.

An exciting blend of history and fiction set in 1916.

17 MARTIN STREET
Marilyn Taylor

Hetty, living in Dublin's 'Little Jerusalem' at the time of the Second World War, hears that a refugee is hiding from the authorities. Can Hetty, her cousin and her Catholic next-door neighbour, Ben, help, or are they just meddling in things they know too little about? Based on a true story.

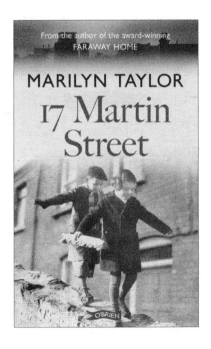